"You don't know the difference between a bull and a cow?" the boy asked, looking curiously at Caroline with his dark brown eyes.

"No," she snapped back. "I do not know the difference between a bull and a cow. And I wasn't about to stop and find out when it was chasing me across the field, either."

The dark eyes inspected her from head to toe. "I reckon you must be the new cousin from the city," he said in a voice that suggested she were a lower life form than an earthworm. He laughed to himself as he turned to walk away.

"Tell Chrissy to stop by later!" he called over his shoulder.

Caroline watched him vault the fence easily, then lope off across the empty field with big, smooth strides. *I guess I did make a fool of myself,* she thought. *But that boy didn't have to be so rude about it! I wonder who he was . . . he was pretty cute. I wonder if I'll see him again. This vacation might be more interesting than I thought. . . .*

Other books in the **SUGAR & SPICE** series:

COMING SOON

Janet
Quin-Harkin's

Sugar & Spice

Nothing in Common

IVY BOOKS • NEW YORK

Ivy Books
Published by Ballantine Books

Produced by Butterfield Press, Inc.
133 Fifth Avenue
New York, New York 10003

Library of Congress Catalog Card Number: 87-90843

ISBN 0-8041-0046-2

Manufactured in the United States of America

First Edition: September 1987

NOTHING IN COMMON

Janet Quin-Harkin

Chapter 1

"You know what I think?" Caroline Kirby asked her cousin Chrissy as the two of them walked together up the last stretch of the hill. "I think winter is finally over."

Down below them, the white buildings of San Francisco spread out in a brilliant panorama. Caroline shaded her eyes and looked beyond to the glittering waters of the bay dotted with white sails, then to the sweeping curve of green hills on her other side, where she could see the afternoon sun reflected in the windows of the houses perched on top. She looked along the edges of the sidewalk at the trees dancing in the breeze with their fragile new leaves. It was the sort of day that whispered beaches and hikes and shorts and picnics, not three hours of homework.

1

Chrissy Madden pushed her blond flyaway hair from her eyes and laughed. "Winter? What winter?" she asked.

"We've had winter," Caroline said, breathing in the fresh spring air. "It rained. It was cold. The wind blew. That's winter."

Chrissy shook her head in disbelief. "Oh come on, Cara. Give me a break! It rained maybe five times, and I had to put on my big jacket a couple of times. That does not get classed as winter. Back home in Iowa my folks were still digging themselves out of the snowdrifts until last month. Now *that* is winter."

Caroline shuddered. "I'm glad I don't have to live through weather like that," she said. "It's quite cold enough for me right here, and I hate the rain. Besides, aren't you glad you didn't have to shovel snow this year?"

"In a way," Chrissy replied thoughtfully, "but when you've had a real winter, you get a real spring."

"We get a real spring here," Caroline said. "What about the cherry blossoms in Golden Gate Park, and the tulips and the wildflowers out on the hills and the green grass?"

"I know," Chrissy agreed. "It's all very pretty, but it's not the same as waking up one morning and noticing that the wind smells different. It has a hint of green about it, if you know what I mean. Then you take a walk, and sure enough, you see the first green shoots sticking up through the snow, and the birds start singing like crazy, and suddenly—wham! All at once it's spring."

"I must say you've gotten very poetic since you started working on the newspaper," Caroline remarked with a smile.

Chrissy shrugged her shoulders. "I always get carried away when I think about home." She stopped walking for a moment and looked at her cousin. "Do you realize that it's almost eight months since I've seen my family and my animals and my boyfriend? Sometimes I worry that they won't even know me when I get home again."

Caroline giggled. "Oh, I can see that," she said. "You'll step off the plane, and they'll say 'Who is that weird creature with the funky shades and the fluorescent T-shirt?'"

"Don't laugh about it," Chrissy protested. "It really worries me."

"It shouldn't," Caroline said gently. "You haven't really changed at all, Chrissy. You may dress a little differently now, but you're still the same loud, crazy person who came here last summer."

"Gee, thanks a lot," Chrissy said, clearly only pretending to be offended. "I thought I'd become refined and sophisticated. In fact I have been working very hard on being a real classy lady. Don't tell me you haven't noticed me walking around school with my nose in the air, talking in my low, sophisticated voice about my Mediterranean cruise. . . ."

Caroline started to giggle again as Chrissy went up the steps to the apartment house ahead of her, wiggling her hips and trailing her hand elegantly along the jasmine spilling over the wall.

"Would you like me to see if there is any mail, dahling?" she cooed in a husky voice.

"Sure, go ahead," Caroline answered through her giggles. She watched Chrissy open their mailbox and reach inside.

"The envelope, please," Chrissy said loudly, bringing out several letters. "And the winner is . . . the electricity bill, how thrilling, my dear, and an advertisement for a stereo sale and . . . *holy cow!*" She twirled around on the small landing, wildly waving an envelope in her hand. "I got a letter from Ben! Yahoo! I got a letter from Ben!" she yelled.

Caroline watched her with amusement. "What were you saying about having turned into a refined and sophisticated person?" she asked, looking at the huge grin on Chrissy's face. "And you thought the folks back home wouldn't know you anymore. They'd recognize that yell clear across the state of Iowa."

Chrissy started to laugh. "Yes, well, it's not every day I get a letter from Ben," she said. "In fact, I haven't had one for over a month. In fact," she went on, her voice becoming suddenly quiet, "I was beginning to get scared that maybe . . . you know . . . he was forgetting about me."

"Oh, Chrissy," Caroline said, putting a hand fondly on her cousin's shoulder. "Who could ever forget about you? I know that even ten or twenty years from now, I'll still remember all the things that have happened since you've been here—like when you took that man's bulldozer to keep him from digging up the park, and dancing in the musical together, and that embarrassing blind date you fixed up for me. In fact, I'll probably tell all these stories to my grandchildren—"

"Would you mind not reminiscing right now? How about finding your key and opening this front door before I die!" Chrissy interrupted, waving the letter in Caroline's face.

"What's the hurry?" Caroline teased, calmly reaching into her purse for her key. "I mean, it isn't as if you have an important letter to read or anything. Are you sure you wouldn't like me to read it to you, while you fix us a snack?"

Chrissy glared. "Caroline Kirby, you are getting as bad as my brothers at teasing. If you're not careful, I will start treating you the way I do them."

"And how's that?"

"I sock them one!"

"In that case," Caroline said, turning the key in the lock, "I think *I'll* make us a snack, and you get to read your letter in private. I'm no match for a girl who used to wrestle hogs!"

She opened the door, and Chrissy sprinted up the stairs ahead of her, two at a time. Caroline followed more slowly, then turned off into the kitchen to make grilled-cheese sandwiches for both of them.

"Chrissy, are you lost in ecstasy, or do you want to come get a grilled-cheese sandwich?" she yelled down the hall minutes later.

There was no answer.

"Well, I'm not letting my slice get cold," Caroline muttered to herself, and sat down in the kitchen to enjoy her snack. She finished her sandwich, poured herself a second glass of milk, and finished that, but still there was no sign of Chrissy.

I bet she's just lying there gazing at the ceiling and murmuring Ben's name over and over, Caroline thought, grinning to herself. *I think I'll take this cheese in to her before it gets disgustingly cold.*

"Chrissy, I'm coming in with your sandwich," she called down the hall. "So come back to earth for a couple of seconds."

She pushed open the door to find Chrissy lying on top of her bedcovers, her blond hair trailing out across the pillow.

"The letter was that good, huh?" Caroline asked, moving the goldfish bowl to the desk so she could set the plate on the dresser. Elvis was swimming around in circles as usual. "You look like your mind is a thousand miles away," Caroline remarked. "I didn't think good old Ben wrote letters like that. I thought they were all about the pigs and chickens."

Chrissy raised herself onto one elbow and looked at Caroline. "Cara," she said, "I want to go home right now."

"Old Ben must certainly have improved in his letter-writing skills, then," Caroline said, still teasing. "So I guess it was a good letter?"

"No," Chrissy said quietly, sinking back with a big sigh. "It was a bad letter."

"Bad news?" Caroline asked, sitting on the bed beside her cousin.

"Terrible," Chrissy said. "Listen to this, will you?" She picked up the sheet of notebook paper and began to read. " 'You'll never guess what Tammy

Laudenschlager decided to do for her Four-H project. She's raising bunnies! I said I'd give her a hand building the cages because she has to get things going in a hurry if she wants some baby bunnies to auction off at the Easter picnic.' "

Chrissy shot Caroline a despairing look. Caroline looked back at her blankly. "Is that the bad news?" she asked, confused. "It doesn't sound too bad to me."

"It's just terrible," Chrissy replied. "It means I'm losing Ben to Tammy Laudenschlager."

"Chrissy!" Caroline said, shaking her head in disbelief. "The guy is only building some cages for her. Does that mean he's getting engaged to this girl back in Danbury? It sounds to me as if he's just being nice and friendly. And he wouldn't have told you about it if he was interested in her, would he?"

"But you don't know Ben," Chrissy said in a despairing voice. "He loves animals—all except rabbits. He thinks they're good-for-nothing, and the wild ones eat his crops. If he's actually building cages for them, he must be really smitten with Tammy Laudenschlager. And you don't know her, either—she'd do anything to get her hands on Ben. She's been chasing him since eighth grade. What am I going to do?"

"Chrissy, I really don't think it's as serious as you think," Caroline said gently. "After all, Ben is only human. If a pretty girl asks him to help her, he's going to do it. You've done things with other boys while you've been here—you can hardly expect Ben to stay at home for a whole year."

"I know," Chrissy said, "and I know it sounds to

you as if I'm worrying about nothing. But you don't
know Ben. It's more the things he doesn't say that
make me suspicious. His last few letters have been
getting more and more distant. They're the sorts of
letters you'd write to a penpal and the name 'Tammy' has been creeping into them. In this one he goes
on to talk about the church picnic right after he
mentions her. That's serious stuff, Caroline."

"What is?" Caroline asked, confused again.

"Talking about Tammy and the church picnic at
the same time," Chrissy said as if the answer were
obvious. "The Easter parade and church picnic are
the first big social events of the year after the winter. It's the sort of thing where a boy shows off his
girlfriend to the whole town. They bid on the pies
the girls have baked, and if a guy bids on your pie,
you know he's interested in you."

"Fascinating," Caroline said. "It sounds like
something out of *Little House on the Prairie.*"

"It's not funny!" Chrissy snapped. "You wouldn't
like it if it was your boyfriend who was going to
bid on Tammy Laudenschlager's pie."

Caroline tried to hide the grin that kept creeping
to the edges of her lips. "I'm sorry," she said. "No,
I'm sure I wouldn't like it. But I still think you're
overreacting. Ben's a nice guy. If he was really
getting interested in this Tammy, don't you think
he'd tell you?"

"Ben's also naive," Chrissy said. "I realize that
now that I've lived among all you sophisticated
types. He probably doesn't even realize that Tammy's chasing him. Before he knows what's happening, she'll have him bidding on her pie, and he'll

be hooked." She lay back and gave a big, unhappy sigh. "I wonder how much it costs to fly home right now? I still have the money Mom sent me for Christmas. Do you reckon your parents would lend me the difference?"

"They might," Caroline answered, "but are you sure it's wise to go rushing back? You might do more harm than good. You might lose your famous temper with Ben and send him right into Tammy Whatsit's arms."

"I've got to risk it, Cara," Chrissy said. "I've just got to go home. I've been missing them all for so long, and I didn't see my family for Christmas, and now my boyfriend is just about to leave me for another girl. I've got to go back, or I'll just die."

"Calm down, Chrissy," Caroline said gently. "We'll talk to my folks tonight and see what we can do, okay?"

Chrissy leaped up from the bed and flung her arms around Caroline. "You are the greatest, you know that?" she said. "I wish I could take you along to tell me what to do about Tammy. You're always so cool and sensible, and you don't fly off the handle like me—" She broke off and stared at Caroline excitedly. "I've got the greatest idea!" she yelled. "If I go back for spring break, why don't you come with me? You could meet all my folks, and I could show you the farm and Danbury, and it would be so much fun! What do you say, Cara?"

"I don't know, Chrissy," Caroline replied cautiously. The idea of spending her spring break in Danbury, Iowa, was not too appealing.

I can see it now, she thought, *three weeks in the*

*middle of nowhere. Of course, the way Chrissy talks
about her farm, you'd think it was paradise, but it's
not exactly the kind of vacation I was looking forward to—especially since it seems I'd be acting as
referee between Chrissy and the dreaded Tammy
Whatsit. I would like to meet Aunt Ingrid, though,
and see where Mom grew up.* She looked at her
cousin's blue eyes, brighter than usual at the possibility of going home and taking Caroline with her.

"We'll talk it over with my folks," Caroline said
finally, "and see what they say."

Caroline's parents thought it was a great idea.
Her mother especially seemed excited about the
prospect of Caroline's visiting her old home.

"You'll be able to see all the places from my
childhood, at last," she said. "And you'll be going
to the Easter Parade and picnic! Why, I remember
when Ricky Anderson bid on the cherry pie that
I'd baked, but when he found a pit in the filling,
he wanted his money back! Oh, and I wonder if
Cousin Alice still makes her poppy seed cake."

Caroline was surprised to notice a slight twang
come into her mother's voice as she talked. She'd
never thought of her worldly-wise mother as a
country girl before. "Do you and Dad have the
money to send both of us to Iowa?" she asked, not
sure if she wanted the answer to be yes or no.

"I'll let you in on a little secret, honeybun," her
mother answered. "You remember that awful
painter we had at the gallery last month?"

"The one who rode bicycles over his canvas and
then tapdanced on it?"

Her mother laughed. "That's the one. Well, his

paintings sold like hotcakes. I got commissions on all I sold, so I'm feeling very rich right now. Besides"—her voice grew wistful—"I'd love for you to visit Danbury and see everything that was so special to me. You'd love the secret place down on the creek. The willows make a little house, and it's just beautiful. Nobody knew about it when we were kids but Ingrid and me. . . ."

Caroline tried to show the same enthusiasm as her mother and Chrissy, but as the day drew nearer she felt more and more tense about the trip. Her friends at school took great delight in teasing her about going to "the boonies," as they put it. They told her horror stories about outhouses full of spiders, farmhouses with no hot water and no electricity, and days full of horrible chores such as shoveling manure and chopping wood for the fire. Although she knew they were only teasing, she couldn't help worrying.

I know I've done more traveling than most girls, she thought, *so I shouldn't be scared about just going to Iowa to see relatives, but I am! The only reason I'm comfortable in places like Paris and Rome is because they are big cities, like San Francisco, but I've no idea what to expect on a farm! I really want Chrissy's family to like me because they are my family, too, and I know it's important to Chrissy and to my mother that they like me. I just wish there was a book at the library called* Fodor's Guide to Farms, *or* How To Talk Farm Talk.

She hid her nerves from both Chrissy and her

mother, as they debated over what to pack and what Caroline should do when she arrived in Danbury.

"She won't have any time to go sight-seeing," Chrissy had said laughingly to Caroline's mother, "because there are a million relatives to visit. Even if we only stay five minutes with each of them, we'll be running around like crazy all the time."

Caroline had overheard this conversation, and it had made the butterflies in her stomach flap their wings even faster. A million new people to meet! Didn't anyone realize what an ordeal that would be for her?

I find it hard enough to talk to new people right here, where we have a lot in common, she thought. *When someone starts talking to me, I just clam up, and by the time I think of the perfect answer, the person has given up and walked away. And I especially don't want to make a bad impression in Iowa. I wish Mom were coming along, because I don't think Chrissy will be any help at all. I'm sure that once she gets back home, she'll rush around being noisy and just being Chrissy, and forget that I exist.*

Caroline Kirby, you are being totally selfish, she scolded herself. *You are not going to Iowa for your own good. You are going to help Chrissy get Ben back from the clutches of Tammy What's-her-name! Your mission is to get Chrissy and Ben back together and to stop Chrissy from murdering Tammy Whatsit, so stop worrying and look upon it as a challenge. And who knows?* she decided, looking at the packed suitcases standing neatly in the hall waiting to be put into the car, *It might also be fun!*

Chapter 2

"Look, Cara, look!"

Caroline drifted out of a pleasant doze to find Chrissy shaking her wildly. She panicked, forgetting where she was for a moment. Then she looked around at the high-backed seats in front of her, and the small window next to Chrissy, and became aware of the constant hum of the plane. She shot awake instantly.

"What is it?" she asked, wondering what Chrissy could find so exciting on a simple plane ride.

"Down there," Chrissy said, dragging her over so she could look out of the window. "See?"

Cara twisted her head so she could look down. Below her, the clouds that had hung over the Rockies had finally cleared, and she found herself looking at what seemed to be a giant checker-

board. Squares of brown joined other squares of
brown, the monotony broken only by an occa-
sional light line of a road or curve of a stream.

"What is it?" she asked Chrissy, "What am I supposed to be looking at?"

"That's Iowa down there!" Chrissy said, loudly
enough for the people in front of them to peer over
their seat backs. "See? Those are cornfields!"

"I don't see much corn," Caroline said.

"Of course not, dummy," Chrissy went on excitedly. "It's only been planted about a month, but
come summer you'll be able to walk between those
fields and have the corn towering over your head."

"As high as an elephant's eye?" Caroline asked
with an amused smile.

"I've never measured an elephant's eye," Chrissy
said, "but it's as high as Ben's head, and that's
pretty high." She grasped Caroline's arm. "Oh,
Cara, what am I going to do? Now we're almost
landing I am so nervous."

"But you have nothing to be nervous about,
Chrissy," Caroline soothed. "You're coming home,
and everyone will be there to welcome you. I'm
the one who should be nervous."

"You?" Chrissy asked. "You don't have a thing
to be nervous about. Everyone will adore you and
make a big fuss of you, and you'll be dragged from
relative to relative, from party to party . . ."

"That's what I'm nervous about," Caroline confessed. "You know how I am with new people."

"But you don't have to feel scared about meeting
people here," Chrissy told her. "We're just plain
folks. You don't have to worry about saying the

right thing or being impressive or sophisticated. You can just say any old thing, and they'll love you just the same."

"If I can just make my mouth say any old thing, I'll be fine," Caroline said with a smile. "My problem is usually that I open my mouth and no sound comes out."

"Then I'll just talk enough for both of us." Chrissy laughed.

"That I can believe," Caroline agreed, laughing with her.

Chrissy's face became serious again. "You'll help me out, won't you, Cara?" she asked. "I mean with Ben."

"With Ben? I bet you'll want me out of the way," Caroline replied.

"It might not be as easy as that," Chrissy said, a frown creasing her forehead. "I've been getting more and more scared, every time I think about it. What if he's not even glad to see me, or he pretends to be glad but then goes off with Tammy and I'm the laughingstock of the whole town?"

"Hey, Chrissy, I'm the worrier in the family," Caroline said softly, patting her cousin's arm. "Don't you start, too. Anyway, in this case I'm sure you've got nothing to worry about. Ben will take one look at you, and any thought of Tammy Whatsit will go right out of his head. Then you and he will wander off together with a silly smile on both your faces, and I can start worrying about what to do on my own for three weeks."

"Then we'll just have to find a nice boy for you

so we can make a foursome," Chrissy said, excited again.

Caroline shook her head firmly. "No, thank you very much!" she said. "I think I'll stick to visiting all the relatives and eating poppy seed cake."

"You'll get enough of that so you'll never want to see another slice," Chrissy exclaimed, "but the rest of the food—oh, Cara, I can't wait to eat real food again."

"Gee, thanks a lot," Caroline said with a grin. "I'm sure my parents will be delighted to hear that we eat pretend food in San Francisco."

"No offense," Chrissy said, "but you guys don't know what real food is—homemade biscuits swimming in gravy and juicy pies smothered in cream and thick ham slices and cornbread stuffing and . . ."

"*Mama mía,*" Caroline said. "I'll go home as fat as a pig."

"No, you won't," Chrissy said. "You'll see. You'll get so much exercise on the farm that after a couple of days you'll be starving for every meal. I wonder what Mom has cooking for supper tonight."

"Nothing too big, I hope," Caroline said. "I never feel like eating after I've been flying."

"Oh, you'll change your mind when you see the food," Chrissy assured her, then let out another loud whoop. "We're coming down! Look, there's a silo! I never thought I'd miss a silo so much . . . and there's a red barn, just like ours, and there's pigs, Cara—look at the pigs!"

"Chrissy, please," Caroline whispered into her ear. "Everyone is turning around to stare at us."

Chrissy looked up at the curious faces with a big grin. "Sorry, folks," she said, "but I've been away from home for eight months. Even pigs look pretty good to me right now."

A ripple of laughter ran through the plane, and Caroline found herself blushing for Chrissy.

Chrissy was still gazing excitedly out the window, not even conscious that other people were looking at her. Outside the window, the brown fields were growing larger and larger. Now Caroline could see the lonely white houses, a few bare trees, an odd patch of green. Wheels bumped against the tarmac, and the plane quivered and slowed, turning from the runway to the terminal building. Caroline looked out with interest at the large modern airport, so different from the dirt strip she had expected.

Chrissy had already gathered up her bag and jacket and was ready to leap off the plane. When the door opened, she took off down the aisle, almost mowing down the people ahead of her. They came out of the gate into a crowded hallway, and several people started yelling and waving in their direction. Chrissy uttered a delighted scream, threw down her bag, and rushed ahead of Caroline, dodging through the crowd to the waving people. Caroline stood there uncertainly, feeling like a piece of unwanted baggage as she saw Chrissy fling herself upon her welcoming committee and be swallowed up with hugs. She picked up Chrissy's bag from the floor and began to walk slowly toward the group, fighting back the frightened feeling that was rising in her throat.

As she got nearer she heard Chrissy say, "Yes, I brought her. She's right . . ." Chrissy's face emerged from the crowd, and suddenly Caroline found several pairs of eyes all staring in her direction. Then a tall, elegant woman with dark hair took a step forward. The woman so closely resembled her own mother that Caroline had to look twice.

"Caroline!" the woman said, stretching out her arms in welcome. "I'd have recognized you anywhere. You're just like one of us—just like your grandma. Come and give your aunt Ingrid a big hug."

Her strong arms almost crushed Caroline in an affectionate hug. "I'm so glad you've come," her aunt murmured into her ear in a voice that sounded dangerously close to tears. "You don't know how much I've been longing to meet Edith's little girl. Now our family is finally whole again."

Caroline looked up and found herself staring into eyes that were clear blue like Chrissy's, yet deeper and wiser and sadder, as if their owner had known a lot of wonderful and tragic experiences and therefore understood a lot of things other people did not. She smiled up at her aunt.

"I'm glad to be here, too," she said. "I've heard so much about all of you."

"Well, I hope you didn't believe all you heard," her aunt said, laughing now. "We're not such a bad bunch when you get to know us." She grabbed Caroline's hand. "Come and meet the troops," she said, leading Caroline toward a big, broad-shouldered man in a plaid jacket and three freckle-faced boys.

"Caroline, this is my dad," Chrissy said, sliding an arm around his waist and nestling her head against his chest. "And I suppose you have to meet my brothers some time, unfortunately."

"Unfortunately for us, you mean," the tallest boy quipped. "We've just had all those months of peace and quiet."

"And we've had the bathroom to ourselves," the middle one added.

Their mother laughed. "You mustn't mind them, Caroline. They are terrible teases, just like their father. This is our oldest son, Thomas." The lanky boy who looked just like a skinny version of his father solemnly shook hands with Caroline. "And this is Will, who is two years younger than Chrissy."

"And just as tall as her already," Will boasted, shooting a delighted glance in Chrissy's direction.

"And I'm Jimmy," said the youngest, staring at Caroline with a pair of brilliant blue eyes fringed with long golden lashes. "I'm nine years old." He turned back to his brothers. "She doesn't look like a weirdo at all."

"Jimmy, hush up," Will scolded.

"But you said everyone in San Francisco was a weirdo," Jimmy insisted.

"I think we'd better get you guys to the car in a hurry," their father said firmly, "before you say any more. Will, take Caroline's bag, and Tom, you can take Chrissy's."

"Has she gotten too weak to carry her own?" Tom asked.

"Thomas Madden. Do what your father says and no backchat," Chrissy's mother said calmly. She slipped one arm around Chrissy and the other around Caroline. "I can't wait to get you girls home and feed you both up. You look like you could do with a good meal—too much of that stupid dieting in the city, I don't doubt."

"I can't wait, either," Chrissy said. "Caroline will tell you how much I've been longing for one of your pies or your biscuits with gravy or your corn-bread stuffing."

"I've got them all made ready for your dinner tonight," her mother said, laughing with pleasure. "I thought you'd be tired after your flight, so I wouldn't let anyone come to join us for dinner. I told Grandma Madden you'd go over there tomor-row, and I told your friends you'd call them in the morning. Jan was calling and Heidi. . . ."

"Did . . . er . . . many of my friends call?" Chrissy asked with a hesitancy that surprised Caroline.

"The phone's been ringing off the hook!" her mother said, giving her a squeeze. "It's okay. The world has not forgotten you."

"Mom wouldn't let us forget you," Will said with a deadpan face. "We were all for renting out your room."

"I don't know why I ever missed you guys," Chrissy retorted, striding out ahead of them.

"Maybe it was our sweet playfulness," Will sug-gested.

"Absence makes the heart grow fonder, Grandma says," Tom added. "We were even looking forward to seeing you again. I don't know why."

"Because she said she'd bring us presents," Jimmy exclaimed, jumping up and down beside Chrissy. "Did you bring us presents? I hope it wasn't weirdo San Francisco clothes."

"That's right," Chrissy said. "You've got it on the nose. I bought you a pink-and-orange flowery sweatshirt."

"Yuck!" Jimmy yelled. "I won't wear it. You didn't really—cross your heart and hope to die?"

Caroline found herself swept along in this noisy, laughing tide of people, out into the fresh air and toward the car. *So this is what a large family reunion is like,* she thought with a mixture of envy and horror as she walked a few steps behind them.

Every now and then one of them would look back at her with interest, although their faces never revealed what they were thinking about her. *I hope they like me,* she thought. *I hope they don't resent having an outsider come home with Chrissy.*

That thought reminded Caroline of the reason Chrissy had first begged Caroline to come along. She was supposed to help smooth things out between Chrissy and Ben—Chrissy's second in the duel against Tammy Laudenschlager. *I hope it doesn't come to that,* Caroline thought, looking around as they approached the flat landscape outside the main airport entrance. *I hate fights, and the last thing in the world I'd want is to be caught in between Chrissy and a strange girl. I hope Ben takes one look at Chrissy and they fall madly in love again!*

Caroline had noticed that Chrissy had not mentioned Ben since they'd landed. She had not even asked if Ben had phoned for her, and that was very unusual for Chrissy. She usually said exactly what she was thinking. *She really must be nervous about meeting him again,* Caroline thought, watching Chrissy's hair swinging across her back as she strode out ahead of her family. *I do hope this trip works out well for her. I hope she's not disappointed. . . .*

Chapter 3

The drive to Chrissy's house took almost two hours, and for Caroline it was two very long hours, crammed into the backseat of an ancient station wagon between Chrissy and Aunt Ingrid. Chrissy talked nonstop, trying to tell her family everything that had happened in the last eight months while at the same time commenting on everything she saw outside the car window.

Caroline couldn't see what was so interesting about the drab, uninviting landscape, but Chrissy seemed fascinated by the row after row of dug-up dirt in the mucky brown fields. *Where's the spectacular springtime Chrissy was talking about?* Caroline wondered. *The only signs I can see of spring here are the patches of new grass growing by the road and the few lonesome plum trees brightening up the countryside with white blossoms. It's so different from the colorful landscapes in California.* Caroline craned her neck to look up at the windmills and silos sticking up metal fingers into the soft evening sky. Even the farmhouses they passed looked isolated and bleak—as if somebody had just plopped a house down on a field several years ago, and nobody had touched it since.

Every now and then the road cut through a small town. The towns all had a sad look about them, as if most people had already moved away. Several of the shops they passed were boarded up, and grass was growing through the cracks on the sidewalks.

"Where has everybody gone?" Caroline asked.

"The small towns don't do much business anymore," her uncle Pete explained over his shoulder. "They used to supply the farmer with everything. Now that everyone has cars and there are decent roads, it's easier for farmers to shop in the big shopping centers. We make a trip into the city maybe once a month, to buy what we need. These little stores can't keep a big-enough stock or low-enough prices to compete. It's a shame—plenty of people I know have had to move away, but that's progress for you."

"Chrissy, you should see the new shopping center over in Charlton," Jimmy squeaked, wriggling around in the hatchback of the station wagon between his brothers. "They have everything you could imagine there. There must be around a hundred different stores."

"You do exaggerate, Jimmy," his mother said, laughing. "There are probably about twenty."

"But there's a big new supermarket," Jimmy insisted. "I bet it's the biggest store you ever saw."

"I don't know," Chrissy said thoughtfully. "Some of the shopping centers around San Francisco and Los Angeles are huge. We've been to a couple that must have twenty different clothing stores just for teenagers."

"Oh, sure," Jimmy said in disbelief.

"Jimmy, you have no idea what a real city is like," Chrissy said.

"I have, too, I've been to Des Moines."

"Jimmy—I mean cities with a million people in them," Chrissy explained. "Houses that go on in every direction. Block after block of skyscrapers and freeways jammed with cars. All those people have to shop and eat—why, I've been to a theater where six different movies were showing at once."

"That's dumb—how can you watch six movies at once?" Will asked scornfully.

Chrissy burst out laughing. "You don't watch them at once, dummy. They are shown in six different little theaters all joined together."

"Well, excuse me," Will growled. "How am I supposed to know, Miss Bigshot? I suppose you think you're too good for us back home now?"

"Of course I don't," Chrissy said. "Just because I'm telling you about the different things I've seen doesn't mean that I think they're better. I'm not trying to put down Danbury. I'd rather have this country road any day than a freeway jammed with cars and all that pollution."

Caroline glanced across at Chrissy, then looked out the window again. She was glad that the boys hadn't put her on the spot the way they had Chrissy. For a moment she felt sorry for her cousin. Chrissy had become accustomed to another world—a world that noone else in her family had ever experienced. Would she ever feel completely at home in Danbury again? *Maybe she should never have come to California,* Caroline thought. *Now she will know all the things she's missing by living here.*

"Oh, look," Chrissy exclaimed as they turned off the highway and onto a narrow country road. "The Johannsens haven't started ploughing yet! How come they've left it so late?"

"Their farm got foreclosed on," her mother said softly. "They've already moved out."

"You mean they've lost their farm—the Johanssens?" Chrissy asked in horror. "But they've lived there for ages. Why, their grandpa was even born there. What happened—did Papa Johannsen get sick?"

"Nothing happened except they couldn't repay the money they'd borrowed," her father explained. "Every farmer around here is in big debt. We all owe money on machines, and we've all had bad harvests, and crop prices have fallen."

"But to turn somebody out of their home—that's just not fair!" Chrissy protested.

"I know, honey," her mother said gently, "but that's the way it seems to be right now. Everybody's fighting to survive these days. They aren't the only farmers who've had to pack up and leave around here."

"But that's terrible," Chrissy said in a broken voice. "I think that's just terrible."

Caroline said nothing. She stared out the window at the unploughed fields and the darkened house beyond. In her safe and secure little world in the city, she had never had to worry about fighting for survival. If her parents lost their jobs, they'd get another one, and if they lost the lease on their apartment, they'd move somewhere else. It was no big deal. But one look at Chrissy's frightened face and she could tell that it was indeed a very big deal. She knew without asking that Chrissy was worrying whether her own family would be next.

But Chrissy was not the sort of person to stay depressed for long. Her mood brightened as they drove through more familiar countryside. She pointed out to Caroline all the little landmarks that had a special meaning for her and related in detail the stories behind each one—to a chorus of groans from her brothers. That ditch was where she had fallen off her bike, and this bend in the creek was where she had fallen through the ice. When she was nine, she had found a stray kitten by this fence, and over there was the orchard where she had gotten caught stealing apples.

By the time they turned onto the rutted dirt track that led to the house, Caroline's mind was in a whirl. How could Chrissy talk so much and so fast? She climbed stiffly out of the backseat. A blast of cool evening air scented with the strange smells of the farm greeted her.

She gazed around at the place that would be home for the next three weeks. The Maddens'

house was bigger than she had expected, with a
gabled roof and a porch running all the way
around. It looked like a friendly house—even the
garden in front was bursting with daffodils, a colorful contrast to the drab Iowa countryside that
Caroline had seen from the car window. To the
left of the house and beyond a grass clearing, she
noticed a big red barn and two wooden sheds surrounded by a wire fence.

"Welcome home, girls," Uncle Pete said warmly.
"Now let's get on inside. You boys can carry in the
bags, and then don't forget about your chores before supper."

"Oh, dad," Will complained. "Does that mean
Chrissy doesn't have to do chores anymore? I've
been feeding her hens since last year."

Aunt Ingrid ruffled his hair playfully. "Give the
girl a break, Will. She's just flown over a thousand
miles. Maybe she'll take over her hens tomorrow."

Just then Caroline heard a loud whoop. "Bonnie,
kitty cats, I'm home!" she yelled, opening the front
door. A big golden dog burst out, leaping at Chrissy and barking hysterically. Caroline hung back
uncertainly and watched as the dog jumped all
over Chrissy, licking her face and howling with
happiness. Then a black-and-white cat and two gin-
ger cats appeared for their turns to be petted and
cuddled.

"And Posey," Chrissy said, leaping down the
porch steps. "I've got to say hello to Posey. I'll see
you in a moment, Caroline."

She disappeared around to the barn. Caroline

looked inquiringly at Will, who was picking up her suitcase.

"Her mare," he said. "She'll probably have to start kissing each chicken individually after that, and then maybe the Mastersons' pigs . . ." A brief grin flashed across his face, and Caroline was pleased to find that she had been included in a family joke. Until now the only time the boys had spoken to her was to answer questions politely.

"Come on in," said Will. "Chrissy will show you to your room as soon as she finishes up with the Wild Kingdom."

Caroline turned to follow him into the house. Jimmy walked beside her, watching her critically. As she reached the door, he commented in his high, clear voice, "You were wrong, Will, she doesn't walk funny."

Caroline felt her cheeks coloring as she glanced back at them. Both Will and Tom were grinning in amusement.

"Who said I walked funny?" she asked.

"Tom said you had one leg shorter than the other and that would make you walk funny," Jimmy said innocently.

"Because of the hills. Tom said that everyone in San Francisco was born with one leg shorter than the other for walking around all them hills."

"We were just pulling his leg," Tom growled, his own face flushing pink as he carried Caroline's bag in ahead of her.

They passed through into a spacious living room filled with solid old maple furniture and with a big fireplace at one end. A staircase on the right led

upstairs, and a passageway in the middle went
back to a big kitchen and eating area. Caroline
sneaked a quick look at the stove and was relieved
to find that it was an ordinary electric one. She
glanced up at the lights and saw that they were
electric, too. This house didn't seem nearly so old-
fashioned as her friends had predicted.

"Caroline, honey, I expect you'd like to use the
bathroom and freshen up a little before dinner,"
her aunt suggested, putting an arm on her shoulder. "I'll show you where everything is." As she
walked toward the back door Caroline's heart sank,
remembering the outhouse and the spiders.

"We've added a second bathroom downstairs
here, if the upstairs one's busy," her aunt said. Caroline breathed a quiet sigh of relief. "Oh, here's
Chrissy now," Aunt Ingrid went on. "Will you show
Caroline to her room, honeybun?"

Chrissy stood in the doorway looking as if she
had just come back from a surprise party. Her
whole face was alight with pleasure. "Everyone re-
members me," she said with a happy sigh. "Posey
and the old rooster and the hens and everybody!
It's so good to be home. Caroline will tell you how
much I missed my animals. I had to make do with
a goldfish called Elvis. He's very sweet, but he
doesn't jump up and lick you."

"More stories over dinner, Chrissy," her mother
insisted. "Take Caroline up, and I'll get dinner right
on the table. I just have to warm up a few things."

Caroline followed Chrissy up the creaking stairs.
The upstairs floor smelled of old polished wood
and pine cleaner. At the far end of the hall, Chrissy

paused in front of a door, then opened it with a flourish.

"This is it! This is my—I mean *our* room," she said. "Nice, isn't it? It's exactly the way I left it."

Caroline stood in the doorway and gazed inside. The room was in one of the gables, so the ceiling sloped down around the window. On the white walls, Chrissy had hung posters of different animals, some with funny sayings. Caroline noticed more animals, this time made of china, on top of the large wooden chest near the door. She followed Chrissy across to the window. Outside, she saw a large tree covered in a mass of white blossom. A cardinal was perched on a nearby branch, his brilliant red feathers contrasting with the frothy whiteness around him.

Caroline nodded in pleasure. "It's a lovely room, Chrissy. I know I'm going to be happy here."

"See this tree, Cara," she explained, opening the window so that the branches almost reached into the room. "This was the tree I told you about. I used to climb in and out of my room this way."

Caroline looked down at the ground, far below, at the very slim branches and the smooth trunk. *"Mon Dieu,"* she said. "I hope you don't ask me to follow you."

Downstairs there was a wild clanging. Chrissy leaped away from the window. "Come on, that's dinner," she said. "Last one down the stairs is a rotten egg!"

Caroline followed as Chrissy bounded noisily down the stairs and ran ahead into the dining room.

Chapter 4

The first thing Caroline noticed when she entered the large, homey dining room was a big table set with a white cloth almost hidden under plates of food. It looked as if Aunt Ingrid was expecting the entire Iowa State football team for dinner. Caroline sat down next to her uncle and smiled shyly at the boys, but they continued to look at her with only cool interest.

I wish I knew what they think of me, Caroline thought. *I want so much for them to like me. After all, besides Mom and Dad, and then Chrissy, this is the first family I've ever had. I wish I knew how to act!*

Aunt Ingrid sat down, and everyone followed as Uncle Pete bowed his head to say grace. As soon as he said, "Amen," eyes snapped open and hands shot out to pass the food around the table.

Caroline tried to protest that she wasn't very hungry as thick slices of ham, huge scoops of candied yams, mounds of vegetables, and hunks of cornbread were heaped onto her plate.

"I really don't think I'll be able to eat all this," she objected as she stared at the pile of food in front of her. "I don't normally have a big appetite, and since we've been traveling, I'm really not hungry at all."

"Nonsense—we haven't given you too much," her uncle said heartily. "Less than that and you'd fade right away. We've got to send you back to your folks in good health, you know. Now eat up— try your aunt Ingrid's famous cornbread!"

How can they do it? Caroline wondered as Jimmy and Tom called for more. *None of them is exactly a blimp. And how do they find time to eat with all the talking?*

That was another thing Caroline found strange. At home when the Kirbys had dinner together, they each spoke in turn and usually in quiet, civilized tones. Tonight Caroline's head was already aching a little from the flight, and she found the noise level at Chrissy's table deafening. It seemed that everybody talked at once, all the time, and as loudly as they could.

"Hey, Chrissy, you should see the Mastersons' new sow. And you know what Luke's doing? He's got a job crop dusting."

"Hey, Chrissy, have you seen the new barn roof yet? It's really great. The snow slips right off it."

"How was the snow this year—pretty bad?"

"Bad? It came clean over the front door. We had to go out the back."

"And guess who Dad made do all the heavy shoveling!"

"I helped, too!"

"Oh, sure—your shovel was about as helpful as a teaspoon. I got the big one."

"So how is Uncle Homer?"

"Better after his surgery. He's looking forward to seeing you. Of course he still walks with a limp, but that's to be expected."

"Cousin Alice said she wants to see you. She thinks you'll be a fallen woman after living in a place like San Francisco. Can you cut me another slice, Dad?"

"Does that mean I've got to stop by at Cousin Alice's too tomorrow? Holy cow! Hey Dad, don't forget about me. I need some more ham, too!"

The conversation and the food passed round and round the table. Caroline sat quietly chewing each piece of cornbread at least thirty times and pretending the yams were not there, by hiding them under her slice of ham.

"Look at Caroline, she's hardly started," Jimmy commented.

"You'll never survive in this family if you don't learn to eat faster than that," Will added.

"Maybe she's not used to the taste of the food," her aunt suggested kindly.

"I guess you're right," Caroline confessed. "And Chrissy will tell you that I have a really small appetite."

She could see the boys looking at her as if she were from outer space, then Will burst out laughing. "What kind of food do they eat in California, then?" he asked.

"We eat a lot of Italian food," Caroline offered. "Chinese food—all sorts."

"No real American food?"

"Hamburgers, I guess."

She could see the boys exchange amused grins. "But I mean food that your ma cooks. What does your ma cook most nights instead of cornbread?"

Caroline could feel her cheeks getting hotter and hotter. "My mother doesn't cook much," she said. "Usually my father does."

This brought a great roar of laughter.

"Remind me never to go to San Francisco," Will spluttered.

"You see, Ma, you should go there if you ever want a break. Find yourself a nice man to cook for you," Tom added.

Caroline could feel her cheeks turning pink with anger and embarrassment. "There's nothing wrong with that," she said in a tight, clipped voice. "It just happens in my family that my mother works outside the home, and she doesn't like to cook anyway. Luckily, my father's a liberated man and not burdened by some ridiculous macho image."

This made the boys laugh even more. She even noticed her uncle joining in.

"Actually, my father doesn't do much cooking," she said. She could hear the superior tone in her voice, but she didn't care. "We eat out a lot. There are so many good restaurants to choose from."

"You eat food in a restaurant?" Jimmy asked, wide-eyed. "Hey, Mom, do you hear that? They get to eat in restaurants. Maybe I'll go live there."

"Don't be dumb, creep. Restaurant food isn't a patch as good as homemade," Will said scornfully. "In those Chinese restaurants they serve up cats and dogs and all sorts of stuff."

"They do not, Will Madden," Chrissy finally intervened. "I've eaten out plenty of times in San Francisco, and the food is real good. I've eaten all sorts of stuff you've never dreamed of. Thai food and Indian and Mexican—you could eat a different kind of food every day for a year in the city."

"Well, I prefer Ma's cooking, even if it is the same stuff night after night," Tom said firmly.

There was an awkward silence, as if they had gone as far as they could go with that subject without being rude.

"Have you eaten all you want, Caroline love?" her aunt asked gently, as if she sensed her panic.

Caroline nodded. "It was very good, thank you, but I'm just not—"

"I understand," her aunt said. "Nobody feels like eating in a strange place after a long journey, but I hope you'll try just one slice of my plum and apple pie."

" 'Hey, how come she gets dessert when she hasn't finished her plate?" Jimmy demanded, scowling across at Caroline. "We never do."

"She's company, stupid," Will growled back. "Company don't have to obey the rules, or do chores or anything."

"Well, I would like you to treat me like one of

the family," Caroline began hesitantly. "After all, we are cousins, and if we'd grown up together, you'd probably treat me just like you treat Chrissy."

"Be thankful you were far away," Chrissy said. "They are the world's worst teases. You can't imagine how lovely it was at Caroline's house without you three brats."

"Sounds boring to me," Will said, giving Tom a wink.

"Yeah, what are families for, except to tease people and keep them in line?" Tom agreed. "If you'd grown up without us, you'd probably be a stuck-up snob who thought she was the cat's whiskers by now." He didn't add, "Like Caroline," but she could tell from the way he glanced in her direction that he was thinking it.

I'll show them, Caroline vowed as she accepted the large wedge of pie smothered with cream that her aunt offered her. Even though she was afraid her stomach might explode if she tried to cram in another mouthful, she forced herself to eat it all. It was truly delicious, but very rich, and she was grateful when the order was given for the children to clear the table.

"Your turn to clean up tonight, Chrissy," Tom commanded. "You already owe us about fifty turns each!"

"It's okay, I'll do it," Caroline said, jumping up from her seat. She was determined to make her cousins like her, even if it meant spending her vacation doing their chores.

"Of course not, Caroline," her aunt insisted.

"You're a guest. We wouldn't hear of it. Those boys will do anything to get out of chores. They're all bone idle."

"But I don't mind helping out at all," Caroline said, picking up a stack of plates. "In fact, I'm looking forward to doing some chores around the farm. It will be fun to collect eggs and things."

As she carried the plates through to the kitchen, Caroline noticed the boys grinning with satisfaction. *When I get home, I'll have to thank Mom and Dad for not giving me a brother*, she thought wryly. *Cousins are bad enough.*

"So, what do you think of the Three Stooges?" Chrissy asked, following Caroline with another stack of dishes balanced precariously on one arm. But before Caroline could think of a reply that would be truthful as well as polite, Chrissy let out a loud gasp. Cara watched helplessly, her hands full, as Chrissy's pile of dishes tottered. The dessert bowl on top slid off, and as Chrissy made a move to catch it with her free hand, the rest of the dishes threatened to topple over. At the last moment, Chrissy let the dessert bowl crash to the floor and used her free hand to steady the large stack instead.

"Phew," she sighed, setting the dishes on the counter. "It looks like I've lost my touch." She grinned at Caroline. "Not that I ever had it, of course."

By the time the girls had finished cleaning up, their eyelids were drooping. They walked up to their bedroom together, leaving behind the sounds of a discussion, competing now with a baseball commentary on television.

"I can't wait to sleep in my own bed," Chrissy said, yawning loudly. "My own dear, comfortable little bed. Of course," she added hastily, "there's nothing wrong with the bed at your house, but my own bed is sort of special. It has this old feather mattress that came from my grandma's house, and it's molded into a little dip in the middle where I always curl up, and the quilt on top Grandma Hansen made when she was a girl. She made the one on your bed, too, so you get to sleep under a quilt that your very own grandmother made."

Caroline looked at the quilt with mixed feelings. She had never known Grandma Hansen, and she had often envied Chrissy for having been so close with her before she died. She had to admit, though, that she found it hard to forgive her grandmother for the way she had treated her mother. What mother would turn out her daughter never to speak to her again, just because she married a man the family didn't approve of? Caroline knew that her own mother would never do a thing like that. Her own mother had always let her choose her own friends, and while she sometimes didn't agree with Caroline's decisions about things, she always let her make her own mistakes. Were people always so narrow-minded out here in the country? She thought of Jimmy's remarks about the San Francisco weirdos and her own wrong ideas about what the farm would be like. *How much damage is done by ignorance,* she thought to herself as she got undressed.

"You'd better get a good night's sleep," Chrissy advised, "because I know we're going to be awakened at the crack of dawn whether we like it or not!"

"Don't worry, sleep won't be a problem," Caroline said, pulling back the covers and climbing into bed. "I'll sleep blissfully the moment my head touches ... Ahhh!" She screamed in horror and leaped out of bed. "Chrissy, there's something cold and slimy in my bed, and it's moving." She shivered and glared at the bed in disgust. "It's alive, Chrissy, I know it is."

Chrissy walked calmly across the room and pulled back the covers. Caroline screamed again as something jumped across the white sheet.

Chrissy laughed. "It's only a frog," she said. "My brothers up to their old tricks again. I thought they would have outgrown kid stuff like that by now. I bet there's one in my bed, too!" She pulled back her own covers and clamped her hand down on the wriggling green creature. "Yup," she said. "Just a welcome-home gift, I suppose. You should feel flattered that you get treated as one of the family."

"Oh, sure," Caroline said, taking a deep breath. "I'm just thrilled to death. Are you sure there was only one?"

"Yeah, they wouldn't bother with more than one," Chrissy said. She slipped her sneakers and jacket on over her nightgown. " 'You go on to sleep, and I'll take these little critters down to the ditch behind the house, poor little things."

Poor little things! Caroline thought angrily. *I*

think she's more concerned about the fright the frogs got than the way I feel.

"Good night, Caroline, good night, Chrissy," innocent voices drifted up the stairs. "Pleasant dreams!"

"No thanks to you creeps," Chrissy yelled back. "Poor old Caroline has nearly died of heart failure, so cut out the dumb stuff or you'll be sorry!"

A roar of laughter echoed up the stairs as Caroline shook out the blankets, then climbed into bed. The bed didn't even feel inviting anymore. It felt cold and slimy and very froggy. She curled herself into a tight little ball.

If that's the way they treat each other in a family, I'm glad I'm an only child, she thought. *I just hope I can survive three weeks here!*

Chapter 5

"Caroline, are you awake?" Chrissy whispered from across the room.

That's a dumb question, Caroline thought. *I've hardly slept a wink all night.*

"Yeah, I'm awake," she replied.

"I'm sorry about Bonnie giving you such a scare," Chrissy said. "She's so used to sleeping on someone's bed. She probably thought she was making you feel at home."

"Well, I'm afraid it had the opposite effect on me. I didn't know what was going on. I woke up to find this heavy body lying across my legs," Caroline said, trying to smile as she remembered her panic. "Then when I tried to sit up, all I could see were these two red eyes, glowing in the dark. Honestly,

Chrissy, I thought it was *Poltergeist Part 3* or *The Amityville Horror!*

Chrissy giggled. "I really am sorry, but I'm also jealous that Bonnie chose your bed instead of mine. She always used to sleep right here." Chrissy patted the foot of her bed. "When you get used to her she'll keep your feet terrifically warm."

"I don't know if I'll ever get used to sleeping in the country," Caroline confessed. "I had no idea the country was such a noisy place."

"Noisy—what do you mean? It's real peaceful out here," Chrissy said, getting up out of bed and stretching her arms wide. "No airplanes flying overhead. No fire trucks waking you up, no cable car bells."

"But you have a hundred other noises instead," Caroline said, rubbing her eyes. "First it was the branches against the window—tip, tap, scritch scratch, all night. Then when I was just dozing off, the house started creaking and cracking."

"I suppose it does," Chrissy admitted, "but I've grown up with it, so I don't notice."

"And then," Caroline went on grimly, "I was finally drifting off to sleep when your rooster started crowing. I'd never heard one up close before. I didn't imagine they'd say cock-a-doodle-doo so loudly and so early!"

Chrissy kept on laughing. "Poor old Cara," she said. "The rooster usually begins around five. That's when my dad gets up. You're lucky we don't keep pigs or geese, like our neighbors. Now *they* really are noisy!"

She walked across to the window and opened it.

A fresh, cool breeze drifted into the room, scented delightfully with blossom and what Chrissy had described as a "green" smell of spring. Caroline smelled it now—a smell that whispered of new, growing things, of ground bursting with life. She shook off her tiredness and got up.

"So what do we do today?" she asked.

"Today is our visiting day," Chrissy answered. "Mom's worked out a schedule that would make the royal family go straight back to bed," she went on. "Every aunt and cousin and neighbor and friend—ten minutes each."

"Does that include Ben?" Caroline asked.

Chrissy frowned. "That rat, Ben. He'd better show up this morning, or he's dead meat."

"Were you expecting him last night?" Caroline asked cautiously.

"At least to phone," Chrissy replied, turning away from Caroline to gaze out the window. "I wrote when I'd be coming back. I bet he was too busy with Tammy Laudenschlager to put the date on his calendar." She shrugged as if it didn't really matter, then slipped on a warm-up suit. "Come on," she said. "You want to help me collect the eggs? We always have to get them before breakfast— before the stupid hens start walking all over them!"

"Oh, sure," Caroline said, jumping up and grabbing her own warm-ups. "That will be fun. That's how I've always imagined a farm—collecting eggs and milking cows and things like that."

"Well, you're too late for the cows," Chrissy said. "My father always does them at five, and they'll be out in the field by now. I'll have to show you the dear little calves we've got in the barn. They are so sweet. It's such a shame they have to be sold."

She ran down the stairs ahead of Caroline, pausing in the hall to take a basket off its hook. "I'll carry this," she said. "You can do the actual finding. That's the fun part."

Bonnie met the girls in the front hall, her tail wagging furiously. Caroline patted Bonnie's soft fur as the dog nuzzled against her legs. She was glad Bonnie had forgiven her for pushing her off the bed during the night. Outside, the air was crisp and cooler than it had been in San Francisco. A light wind was blowing, and the sky was streaked with pinkish clouds.

"Doesn't look too promising for the Easter picnic on Sunday," Chrissy said, frowning up at the sky.

"What happens if it rains?" Caroline asked.

"Oh, they hold it in the church hall, but that's not as much fun. It's too crowded, and nobody gets a chance to parade their hats or their horses," she said, "Hopefully the rain will blow over by then. Weather changes real fast in this part of the world."

They crossed the yard and walked past the new barn. Beside it was a long, low house surrounded by wire, and an even smaller house was beside that.

"This is the chicken run," Chrissy said, "and the little house is the incubator. Most folks go into town and buy chicks ready-hatched these days, but Ma still likes to do her own. She says it gives her a feeling of satisfaction to watch all those little fluffy bundles climbing out of their eggs. Most of them have already hatched by now. I'll show you them later." She leaned over and opened the wire-mesh gate to the chicken run. "First we'll visit the hens. They're not as cute as the chicks, but we have to keep the chicks in the incubator for the first couple of weeks, until they get big enough to put out with the hens."

As soon as Chrissy pulled open the henhouse door, a flock of hens scurried eagerly out onto the chicken run and gathered around the girls, clucking all the while.

"They think we've got food," Chrissy said. "Tom will bring out their hot mash in a minute. Now you go on inside and see how many eggs you can find. Look in the most unlikely places—they never lay eggs in their boxes!"

Caroline reluctantly ducked in through the small doorway and crouched inside the smelly henhouse. Several hens perched near the door edged away from her and hid in the corner. Others looked defiantly from their nests.

"Nice chickens," Caroline said, realizing as she said it that she sounded stupid. She looked around for eggs but didn't see any. She could hardly go back out to Chrissy empty-handed. That would just be one more thing to make her look stupid. She bent down cautiously on the straw-covered floor and began to rummage around. Her efforts produced an egg almost immediately.

"I've got one," she called triumphantly. "Oh, and I see another—right under . . ." Her voice trailed away as she found herself looking into the beady eyes of an enormous rooster. Caroline had never seen a real rooster before, but there was no mistaking him for a hen. What's more, he was making threatening little clucking noises in his throat as if daring her to pick up the egg. As Caroline looked around for a graceful way to back out, she noticed that the other chickens had come inside again and were standing around her in a circle. Chickens weren't dangerous animals—were they? She could feel sweat running down the inside of her warmup suit, especially when she noticed that the way to the door was blocked solidly by hostile chickens.

"Chrissy?" she called softly, trying not to provoke an attack. "Chrissy, could you get in here a minute?"

At that moment a hen fluttered down from a perch above and landed on the back of Caroline's neck. She didn't stop to think but screamed in panic and waved her arms wildly in the air. The chickens scattered, and Caroline ran outside.

"What on earth happened?" Chrissy asked, helping her cousin away from the henhouse. At the very same moment Will emerged from the house while Tom came running around the barn. "What's going on?" they demanded. "What happened to her?"

"The—the chickens," Caroline stammered. "They started to attack me. They got in a circle around me and the rooster came and then one landed on my back!"

She looked at the grins on her cousins' faces and bristled. How could they think this was funny?

"Attacking chickens?" Tom asked.

"It hooked its claws into the back of my neck," Caroline insisted.

"That's because it thought you had some food," Chrissy explained gently. "That's why they clustered around you. They were waiting to be fed."

"I thought they were planning to eat me for breakfast," Caroline said miserably.

The other three burst out laughing at this. "I never yet met a man-eating chicken," Will said to Tom.

"How was I to know anything about chickens?" she said coldly, brushing feathers and straw out of her hair. "Where I come from, we buy eggs in civilized supermarkets." Then she turned and stalked back to the house.

A few minutes later Chrissy followed her. "Don't feel too bad about being teased," she said kindly. "We couldn't help laughing at the way you looked. I'm sorry. It must have been scary for you."

"It was," Caroline said, looking away from her cousin. "This great big rooster came right up to me, and when I tried to back away, the other chickens surrounded me. When one landed on me I thought they were starting to attack!"

Chrissy's mother was very comforting when she heard the story. "Those boys had no right to laugh. I'd like to see them fend for themselves in the big city," she said, frowning in their direction as they helped themselves to huge stacks of pancakes. "They'd be scared silly just trying to cross the street, I bet."

"Oh, come on, Ma," Tom said as he poured

oceans of syrup over the pancakes and then topped it with slices of ham.

"You have a good breakfast and don't worry about them," Caroline's aunt said, putting an arm around her shoulder. "Afterward you and Chrissy have got some visiting to do, and you need your strength."

Caroline was about to say that she hardly ate any breakfast at home, but she saw her cousins' scornful stares as they crammed in huge mouthfuls, so she accepted the pancakes and ham and found, to her surprise, that she could finish the whole plateful. What's more, everything tasted good, including the milky coffee and the thick maple syrup, so different from the pale runny stuff sold in store bottles.

"I won't offer you an egg today, Caroline," her aunt said, smiling. "I have the feeling you've seen enough of them for a while. But if you'd like, maybe after breakfast Chrissy will show you my little pride and joys in the incubator. If you're lucky enough, you'll see one hatch."

When they finished eating, the two boys disappeared out to the farm with their dad, and Chrissy took Caroline over to the incubator.

"Now these are the sorts of animals I feel comfortable with," Caroline said, peering delightedly at the yellow bundles of fluff that ran about cheeping. "Such a pity they grow up to be those horrible hens!"

"We're in luck," Chrissy said, pointing to an egg near the heater. "This one's trying to get out."

As they watched, they saw a little hole in the

egg and a tiny beak pecking at it from inside. Caroline felt that she was experiencing a miracle as gradually the egg cracked and then a damp, skinny little chick fought to break out of the shell. At last he was free, except for a piece of shell balanced on his head. He stood there, as if modeling a new sort of hat, but looking very sorry for himself, until the girls took pity on him and removed the last piece of shell.

"Next time you see him he'll be all soft and fluffy like the rest," Chrissy said. "In fact—" She broke off as they heard a loud honking outside.

"Ben!" she yelled delightedly. "It's Ben, Cara!" And she flew ahead of Caroline out of the incubator, leaving Caroline to close the door behind them.

Caroline rounded the barn to see a battered red truck drawing to a halt in the dirt driveway. She had already seen Ben in plenty of pictures, but she was not prepared for the real thing. Chrissy had said he was a football player, and that was exactly what he looked like. He climbed out of the truck, standing to well over six feet with broad shoulders and well-formed muscles. He pushed a fringe of light blond hair back from his forehead as he walked toward Chrissy.

"Hi, Chrissy," he said.

Chrissy walked toward him. "Well, look who's shown up at last," she called.

Caroline noticed the beaming smile drop from Ben's face. *Why isn't Chrissy acting happy to see him?* Caroline wondered. *She'll lose Ben for sure if she keeps on like that.*

"What do you mean?" Ben asked. "Your ma said

I wasn't to bother you yesterday, as you'd be tired out from the flight—although how sitting still doing nothing for four hours makes anyone tired, I can't figure."

"But you could have called," Chrissy said.

"I took it to mean that not bothering meant not calling, too," Ben answered.

"Well, I guess you have other things on your mind right now," Chrissy said in a cool voice. "Other fish to fry—like Tammy Laudenschlager?"

"What is this, Chrissy?" Ben demanded. "Do I have to go through the third degree before I get a welcome-home kiss? Didn't you miss me all this long time—because I sure as heck missed you. I've been waiting and waiting for this moment, and now you're all set to spoil it."

Chrissy's face softened. "I don't want to spoil it, Ben," she said, taking a step toward him. "I've been waiting for it, too."

"Then get over here and quit stalling, girl," Ben said. "Come and give me a great big kiss!"

He swept Chrissy into his arms, and they clung together. Caroline shrank back against the barn, feeling like a peeping Tom and yet unable to move away without being seen. Suddenly, Chrissy broke away from Ben's embrace and turned toward Caroline.

"Hey, wait a minute, you've got to meet my cousin Caroline—the one I stayed with back in California. She's come to see what country living is like."

As Ben turned his glance toward her, Caroline was conscious of piercingly blue eyes that crinkled at the sides in a friendly way when he smiled. He shook her hand with a firm grip. "Pleased to meet you, Caroline," he said, "and I want to thank you for taking good care of Chrissy for me."

"It was nothing," Caroline mumbled as she tried to think of a good exit line. Chrissy certainly wouldn't want her around now, she was sure.

"I'll go and finish unpacking," she said. "I'm sure you two have a million things to talk about."

Chrissy and Ben grinned at each other.

"Want to go for a ride in the truck?" Ben asked.

"You bet," Chrissy said. "I won't be too long, Caroline, because we still have a lot of visiting to do today. Make yourself at home. Go visit my mare or the calves in the barn."

"Don't worry about me, I'll be just fine," Caroline said. "As long as I stay away from the chickens." She smiled at Chrissy as her cousin climbed up into the truck beside Ben. As they drove off in a cloud of yellow dust, Caroline watched them go with a tinge of jealousy. How nice it must be to have a boy wait all that time for you. *Chrissy had better appreciate Ben*, she thought. *I wonder if I'll ever have a special boy like that. I thought Alex was special, but that didn't go on forever. And I really liked Jimmy, but we didn't have much in common. Never in my whole life have I met a boy who makes me feel that I could touch the moon.*

She turned her eyes away from the disappearing red truck and headed back for the barn, determined to keep herself busy and not think about Chrissy and Ben.

"I think I'll look at the sweet little baby calves first," she told herself.

She approached the barn door and opened it cautiously. In the dim light she could see the outlines of four baby calves, standing around a full manger. As she stepped inside, she realized that there was another animal in the barn besides the calves. Out of the darkness on her left, a huge shape came lumbering toward her. For a moment she stared at the enormous head, the big curved horns, the snorting breath. Caroline had never seen a bull close up before, but she knew that she was looking at one now. The bull trotted toward her, and she could feel the heat of its snorting breath. Without waiting another moment, she turned and fled.

Out into the bright sunlight she ran. She hadn't had time to shut the barn door, and she could hear the bull right on her heels.

"Help!" she called. "Help, the bull's loose!" Her one aim was to escape the fierce animal that was following her. She sprinted across the farmyard and toward the fence surrounding a large vegetable garden. She made for it with the last of her strength and vaulted over it. Behind her she could hear the pounding hooves of the bull, thudding on the packed earth. Where was everyone? Why didn't anyone hear her calling? Then a dreadful thought sneaked into her mind. Was the bull a trick played by her horrible cousins? They had heard Chrissy say that Caroline should visit the calves— had they sneaked a bull into the barn just to give her a fright?

Serve them right if they have to go round him

up, she thought, taking a deep breath to stop herself trembling.

"Tom! Will!" she yelled. "The bull's out." Caroline was calmer now. She'd never let those boys know how scared she was of the large, angry animal eyeing her from the other side of the fence.

Finally she saw a tall figure racing across the bare field. She realized with a start that it was not one of her cousins. This boy had dark hair and wore a black leather jacket. He vaulted the fence between them and drew level with her, panting. "Were you the one yelling? Where did the bull go?" he demanded. "Where's Mr. Madden? You'd better find him and tell him to get the truck." He gazed right through Caroline as if she didn't exist, his eyes scanning the empty fields.

Caroline looked at the boy in confusion, for he was standing not five feet away from the bull.

"But it's right here," she said, pointing to the large horned head leaning over the fence toward her.

Now it was the boy's turn to look at Caroline in confusion.

"I thought you said the bull was loose," he said. "Is this some kind of dumb joke?"

"What's that, then?" Caroline asked, stepping back as the bull snorted violently.

"Looks like Blossom to me," the boy said matter-of-factly. "The old cow they keep in the barn to provide milk for the new calves."

"Oh," Caroline said, feeling her cheeks grow warm. "Well, it looked like a bull to me."

"You should look a little more closely before you

go yelling and scaring folks for nothing," the boy advised, looking at her curiously with his serious chocolate-colored eyes. "Don't you know the difference between a bull and a cow?"

Caroline turned back to the large brown animal again and noticed, for the first time, the large, dangling udder. "No," she snapped back. "I do not know the difference between a bull and a cow—at least not from the front end. Where I come from it's not a necessary tool for survival. And when a large pair of horns charged at me in the dark, I didn't wait around to do a thorough inspection!"

The dark eyes looked her up and down. "I reckon you must be the new cousin from the city," he said with disdain, as if she were a life form lower than an earthworm. "Lucky for you I was out in the south pasture, or you might have been licked to death by a too friendly cow." He laughed to himself as he turned away again. "Tell Chrissy to stop by later," he called over his shoulder.

Caroline watched him vault the fence easily, then lope off across the empty fields with big, smooth strides. When he was out of sight, she climbed back over the fence and cautiously approached Blossom. She put her hand out to the cow, then stood very still as Blossom licked her palm. How stupid she had been to think this gentle animal could be a vicious bull.

"You wouldn't hurt a fly, would you, Blossom?" she said softly as she led the big cow back to the barn. "I guess I did make a fool of myself, but that boy didn't have to be so rude about it. I wonder who he was?"

Chapter 6

Caroline spent most of the morning upstairs. She figured that at least she would be able to avoid any more mishaps if she stayed in her bedroom. As she lay on top of her grandmother's quilt, soothed by the gently fluttering lace curtains and the constant clucking of the hens, she felt tiredness overtake her. She had almost drifted off to sleep when she was roused by the sound of an approaching motor. From her window she watched Ben's red truck come to a halt. Chrissy sprang down almost before it had stopped, then she ran into the house without looking back while the truck drove away with tires spinning. It didn't take the world's greatest detective to deduce that something was wrong.

Chrissy clomped noisily up the stairs, and seconds later the door burst open and in she came.

Her cheeks were flushed pink, and her eyes were unnaturally bright and rimmed with red.

"Well, that's it," she said in a tight little voice. "It's all over and finished. We might as well go back to San Francisco right now."

"Chrissy, what happened?" Caroline asked in concern.

"I guess I've just broken up officially with Ben," Chrissy said, as if she were still fighting to stay in control.

"B-but Chrissy," Caroline stammered. "He seemed so pleased to see you this morning. What went wrong?"

"What went wrong was Tammy Laudenschlager," Chrissy replied, picking up her brush and pulling it savagely through her hair as she stared into her vanity mirror. "I guess I'm not generous enough to want to share Ben with another girl."

"Is that what Ben said?" Caroline asked. "He wanted you to share him with Tammy Whatsit?"

"Not exactly," Chrissy said angrily. "But he did confess he'd taken her out while I was away and that he'd probably take her out again after I went back."

"But Chrissy, you've been out with other guys in San Francisco," Caroline reminded her cousin. "What about Hunter? What about Jay?"

"That was different," Chrissy said airily. "It didn't matter about them because nobody knew. In a little town like this everybody knows. I'll never be able to show my face again."

There was a long silence.

"So I guess that's that," Chrissy said with a shrug.

"Maybe it was a good thing. Maybe it's about time I moved on. After all, who wants to be tied to a farmboy jerk?"

There was another silence. Chrissy went on brushing her hair, even though it was now shining and tangle free. Caroline was surprised at Chrissy's quiet acceptance of the breakup. She would have expected exactly the opposite—but she doubted that Chrissy was feeling so calm inside.

"Chrissy," she said at last, "is that what you really want? Are you really prepared to lose Ben forever, just because the town might gossip about him being seen with Tammy? Does what other people think mean that much to you—does it mean more than Ben? You should think this over really carefully, you know, because you are just giving up three years of a relationship for one silly quarrel."

She could see Chrissy's big eyes in the mirror and could tell she was wavering. Then Chrissy tossed back her hair and turned toward Caroline. "Anyway, it's too late now," she said, "because I really blew it. I've just told Ben I never want to see him again."

"What on earth made you do that?" Caroline asked, looking with sympathy at her cousin.

"Because I'm dumb, I guess," Chrissy said, sinking onto her bed opposite Caroline. "You know me—I never was too famous for my calm nature. When Ben told me about the church picnic, I guess I sort of exploded."

"You exploded? Over what?"

"He asked if I'd mind if Tammy went with us, too, and I told him that if Tammy was coming, I wasn't."

"Is this church picnic a real boy/girl thing?" Caroline asked. "Or is it more like a bunch of friends having a good time?"

"Well, sort of both. I told you already about all the girls auctioning off their pies. It seems that Ben had already promised to bid on Tammy's pie, before he knew that I was coming back for the picnic."

Caroline fought back a desire to giggle. This whole thing seemed so ridiculous. She could just imagine Laura Ingalls auctioning off a pie in *Little House on the Prairie.* Fighting over who bid on your pie seemed crazy, but Chrissy was obviously taking it very seriously.

"Does it matter that much if Ben bids on another girl's pie?" she asked cautiously.

Chrissy's cheeks flamed scarlet again. "Does it matter?" she asked as if Caroline had questioned whether it was important if a boy got engaged to two girls on the same day. "When a boy bids on a girl's pie, the whole town knows he's interested in her. Ben said he was only doing it because Tammy felt bad last year that nobody had bid on her pie and she had begged and begged him, but I don't swallow that too easily. He also said that he wouldn't have even suggested meeting Tammy there if he'd known I'd be back."

"Well, there you are, then—you're still number one, what more do you want?" Caroline asked.

"I don't want to be number one," Chrissy said angrily. "I want to be number only."

"So now it looks like you're number zero," Caroline said. "Are you happy about that?"

"Of course I'm not happy," Chrissy snapped. "I'm so miserable I could cry my eyes out, but that Ben Hatcher has got to be taught a lesson. He's got to be taught that nobody two-times me!"

"And what if he decides he prefers Tammy?" Caroline asked. "You remember what happened with me and Alex, don't you? I didn't have time for him, so he turned to the girl who did."

Chrissy sat on her bed, looking down at the rag rug on the floor. "I don't want to lose Ben, Caroline. I really don't." As Caroline watched, a big tear trickled down Chrissy's cheek. She looked so sweet and helpless that Caroline wished she had a magic potion to bring Ben back.

"I don't know what made me act like that, Cara," Chrissy went on, swallowing a sob. "Ben was so happy to see me, and I behaved like a jerk. Everything he said I attacked. I guess I've always been so sure of him before. I just don't know how to handle this jealousy."

"Then phone him up and tell him you're sorry," Caroline suggested.

"I can't do that," Chrissy replied miserably. "You don't know what terrible things I said to him. It was as if I couldn't control my mouth and some horrible person was speaking through me. I doubt that he'll ever want to see me again."

"Maybe you're blowing things up," Caroline consoled. "Maybe when you've both had a chance to calm down, he'll realize you're the one he wants after all."

"I hope so," Chrissy said, sniffing loudly. "I can't

believe how dumb I was. Do you think jet lag can addle a person's brains?"

Caroline smiled. "Maybe."

Chrissy sniffed again, then got up and walked across to the window. "Well, at least you won't have to worry about me being away with Ben during this vacation," she said. "I'll be able to be with you all the time and show you around."

"Well, that's one good thing," Caroline said, "because I don't think I'd survive these three weeks on my own."

Chrissy looked around in horror. "Why on earth not?"

"Because the farm is full of dangers for people like me. You remember how you got swept away by waves and nearly fell off cable cars? Well, I've already been scared by chickens and frogs and chased by bulls . . ."

"Chased by bulls?" Chrissy looked bewildered. "But we don't have a bull. The nearest bull is over on the Phillips farm six miles away."

Caroline slid off her bed and went to stand beside Chrissy at the window. "I thought it was a bull, but it turned out it was only Blossom," she admitted.

"Old Blossom?" Chrissy said, grinning through her tears. "Did she chase you?"

"She sure did. I heard the pounding hooves and saw those huge horns, and I didn't wait around to see if it was a cow or a bull."

Chrissy looked amused. "I guess with her horns Blossom might look pretty scary. Normally we clip the horns off all the calves, but we got Blossom when she was already full-grown," she explained, then started to laugh. "Poor old Cara. You've had quite a morning. We both have. Things can only get better after this, can't they?"

"I hope so," Caroline said.

"I wonder if I should find another boy to take me to the church picnic? To make Ben jealous, I mean?"

"I don't know, Chrissy," Caroline said. "I'm not a great person to ask about boys. But if you decided to do that, I can think of a candidate for you. A boy already came over to see you this morning."

"He did?" Chrissy asked, her face lighting up instantly. "Who?"

"I didn't exactly get his name, but he came over the fields from that direction, and he has big dark eyes and he's very tall."

"Oh," Chrissy said, her face falling again. "That's only Luke."

"Luke?"

"Yes, Luke Masterson, our neighbor."

"The one with the pigs?"

"That's right. We've grown up together. He's just like another brother. Did he come over here looking for me? That seems very strange."

Caroline blushed. "He came over because he heard me calling for help," she confessed, "but I think he was heading over here anyway. He asked you to stop by later."

"That probably means his mother sent him to ask me to stop by," Chrissy said. "He's a worse tease than my brothers are. We usually stay well away from each other."

"I think I'll be joining you in staying well away," Caroline said, grinning in embarrassment. "He told me how dumb I was not to know a cow from a bull."

Chrissy nodded. "That's Luke for you—always telling you exactly what he thinks of you, even if you don't want to hear it."

"He seemed just plain rude to me," Caroline remarked.

Chrissy shook her head. "Boys—what a pain," she said with a mischievous grin. "Don't you think the world would be a better place without them?"

Caroline thought for a moment, remembering her best days with Alex. "No," she said firmly.

"Me neither," Chrissy said, laughing. "Oh, Cara—what am I going to do to get Ben back? We've got to think of something!"

Chapter 7

The next couple of days were a blur of frantic activity for Caroline. Chrissy dragged her from one friend or relative to the next, talking nonstop all the time until Caroline's head was swimming with aunts and uncles and cousins and cousins of cousins. Caroline realized that keeping busy was Chrissy's way of dealing with her fight with Ben, so she tried her best to keep up with the hectic schedule and to cheer up her cousin.

"I thought the sign said Danbury, population three hundred and fifty," she remarked as she and Chrissy trudged home beneath the setting sun. "We have seen at least a thousand people today, and we've walked at least a thousand miles!"

Chrissy managed a smile—something she hadn't done since the fight with Ben. "I thought I was supposed to be the one who exaggerated!" she said. "Since Mom gave us a lift to town, we only ended up walking a few miles, and we've only seen a couple of relatives!"

"A couple of relatives!" Caroline sighed. "Chrissy, I've met Uncle Homer and Cousin Dutch and Jerry and Betsy and Auntie Trudy and Heidi and Jan, and I'm sure there were millions more, but my mind has gone blank."

"I thought you wanted to meet your long-lost relatives," Chrissy said.

"I did—I mean, I do," Caroline agreed, "but not in five-minute sessions. I'm not even clear which ones were my relatives and which ones were your father's family."

"Cousin Dutch is yours, so are Jerry and Betsy," Chrissy said smoothly. "Uncle Homer is really Dad's uncle. Heidi and Jan are just friends."

"And what about Auntie Trudy?"

"She nobody's relative. We just call her Auntie because she was Grandma's friend."

"Grandma Madden's friend?"

"No, Grandma Hansen—your grandma," Chrissy said.

The words gave Caroline the same odd feeling that she'd experienced when Chrissy had told her that her grandmother had made the quilt on her bed. She wondered what Grandma Hansen was like, but she wasn't sure that she would have wanted to meet a woman who could disown her own daughter. But from the way Chrissy talked about her, it was clear that Chrissy had adored her.

"I wish you'd known Grandma Hansen," she said.

"She was so pretty—she looked a lot like you. She kept her blond hair real long right until she died, and she never tinted it, either, and she used to tell lovely stories when we were little, and she had a secret jar of peppermint candy we always used to find. . . ."

Caroline stared wistfully at the big red barn up ahead, wishing she'd had somebody to tell her stories and gives her forbidden candies when she was little. "Well," she said, "maybe you'll let me share Grandma Madden."

"You really liked her, didn't you?" Chrissy asked. "I could tell you two hit it off right away."

"She is really special," Caroline said, picturing the tough little old lady whose skin looked like leather but whose eyes still sparkled like a young woman's. "It was so easy to talk to her."

"So I heard," Chrissy said, shooting Caroline a quick look. "Those walls are not too thick, you know. I heard you two talking about me and Ben."

"I'm sorry," Caroline said. "I didn't mean to talk about you behind your back. She was the one who brought it up. Apparently she knew all about it— did you tell her?"

Chrissy smiled bitterly. "News gets around real fast in a place like this," she said. "So what did Grandma say—about me and Ben, I mean?"

Caroline smiled. "She said you both had too much pride, and you'd never get back together unless somebody threw you back together."

Chrissy laughed. "Was she suggesting you do the throwing?"

"I gather she was," Caroline admitted. "I had to tell her I'm a rotten thrower."

"So did she have any other suggestions?" Chrissy asked hopefully.

"Chrissy," Caroline said with a sigh, "if you really want him back, call him up and talk to him. Tell him you were jet-lagged, tell him your cousin is a bad influence on you if you like, but just let him know you're sorry."

Chrissy's face suddenly flushed very pink. "You know I can't do that, Caroline," she said in a tight voice. "I'm not crawling back to him or to any boy. I wasn't the one who started it—he should never have gone with Tammy Laudenschlager in the first place, even if I was away."

Caroline opened her mouth to say something, then closed it again. Chrissy could really be unreasonable sometimes. She certainly wasn't seeing Ben's side of things in this case, and Chrissy was a hard person to tell things to, especially when she was being extra stubborn like now. Grandma Madden had told Caroline as much while they got tea ready in the kitchen that afternoon. "That girl will just have to learn the hard way," she said. "It's no use telling her a thing, but, between you and me, if she wants that boy back, she's going to have to fight for him. He's not the type of boy to come running back just because she snaps her fingers!"

Caroline had a feeling that Grandma Madden was right. *Chrissy had better shape up,* she thought, *or she'll be sorry.*

As the girls walked silently around the barn toward the house, Caroline happened to turn her gaze upward. She stopped still in her tracks and opened her eyes wide in wonder at the spectacular evening sky. It looked as if a mad painter had streaked the sky with glowing shades of pink and purple and blue. She watched as an ugly gray cloud rapidly approached the brilliant streaks of color and swallowed them up. She shook herself back to reality and the problem at hand.

"Well, I guess Grandma Madden was right," she said, patting Bonnie, who had run out to greet the girls.

"About what?" Chrissy demanded.

"She said it was a good thing you had decided not to go to the church supper, because there was no way your pie would get as high bids as Tammy's."

"Grandma said that?" Chrissy yelled.

Caroline nodded as she walked toward the house. "She said the way you baked, Ben would be a fool not to choose Tammy's pie over yours."

"I don't believe you," Chrissy said angrily.

"How would I make something like that up?" Caroline asked, pushing open the front door. "I don't know anything about pie-baking contests. The whole thing sounds really dumb and provincial to me. If I liked a boy and I fought with him by mistake, I'd try and tell him I was wrong, but I guess out here women have to win back their men by baking the best pie."

Chrissy pushed through the door after her. "Mom, do you have any of last year's peaches left?" she yelled as she walked through into the kitchen. "I have some baking to do!"

Caroline grinned as she heard Chrissy clattering desperately around the kitchen. *I don't think I'll ever understand her completely,* she thought. *It's a good thing Mom moved to San Francisco and I wasn't born out here. I'd never be the type of person to try to win back a boy in a pie-baking contest! I just hope Chrissy lets Aunt Ingrid help her, because she'd never win back anyone with her cooking!*

In spite of everyone's predictions of rain on Easter Sunday, Caroline woke up to a crisp, bright morning. The sky was a delicate light blue, with a few puffy white clouds scudding past. Although a strong wind blew across the fields, nobody seemed to mind.

After a church service that lasted until noon, Caroline and the Maddens walked down Main Street toward Grandma Madden's house. Caroline privately thought Main Street was a funny name for this quiet country road. There was a gas station here, and a small grocery store, a feed lot on the railway line, the police and fire stations, Danbury Elementary and High schools, and a few neat little houses behind white picket fences—and that was the whole of downtown Danbury.

As they neared Grandma Madden's, Caroline noticed several cars parked in the driveway, and through the large picture window she could see a crowd of vaguely familiar faces.

"Who else is having lunch at your grandmother's?" Caroline asked Chrissy nervously.

"The whole family. We do it every Sunday after church," Chrissy replied.

"The whole family?" Caroline looked horrified.

Chrissy giggled. "Not everyone. Just Cousin Homer and Cousin Beth, and their daughter and her children, and old Cousin Alice . . . you remember the famous poppy seed cake! That's it. Oh, and us and Grandma. Usually around fourteen people, that's all."

"Oh, I see," Caroline said. She swallowed her panic at the thought of being with fourteen strangers. She had already met most of these people during Chrissy's whirlwind tour, but then she'd only had to smile and accept a cup of coffee. Now she was afraid she'd have to answer all kinds of questions. It seemed as if living in a big city were strange enough to people in Danbury, but California might as well have been another planet!

"Here they are at last, here's our world traveler!" Uncle Homer boomed heartily as Caroline followed Chrissy into the house. "And here's the little lady from the city—you come and sit by me, little lady. I've got lots of things I want to find out from you."

Caroline's heart sank as Uncle Homer escorted her firmly to the table set up in the dining room and helped her onto a piano stool, then squeezed himself into the chair beside it.

"Let's get on with it, then, Effie," he called to Grandma Madden. "Everyone's wasting away for lack of food."

It didn't look to Caroline as if anyone at the table were in great danger of wasting away, but Grandma Madden started bustling around twice as fast, bringing out dish after dish from the kitchen with help from Chrissy and her mother. Caroline hoped she didn't looked lazy or snobbish, perched on her piano stool, but Uncle Homer had her trapped.

As everyone wriggled in around the crowded table, talking and laughing nonstop, Caroline felt as she had the first night at the Madden's. She was an outsider here and was acutely aware that she did not belong.

Even Uncle Homer did not pay much attention to her once the meal began. He asked her how she liked Danbury and then started up a conversation across the table with Chrissy's dad about the fuel line in a new harvester. So Caroline sat in the corner, watching and listening. In a way, she was relieved not to have to say anything. At least this way, nobody could laugh at her. Chrissy was quiet, too, Caroline noticed, and she hardly ate a thing. She kept glancing up at the clock as if she couldn't wait for the parade and the picnic, but Caroline knew her cousin well enough to realize that she was very nervous.

"Baked your pie yet, Chrissy?" Uncle Homer called loudly down the table.

"She's not going, Homer, don't you remember a thing?" Grandma Madden reminded him firmly.

"I changed my mind, Grandma," Chrissy said, flushing as she spoke. "I decided I would go after all—for Caroline's sake, you know. She's never seen anything like our church picnic. They don't have stuff like that back in San Francisco."

"No, I suppose it's all nightclubs and discos and

such things back there," Cousin Alice remarked.
"The things you see on television—the shootings
and the muggings. It's a wonder you got back
safely, child."

Caroline saw Grandma Madden's bright eyes
catch Chrissy's through the noisy discussion. "It's
good of you to go, for Caroline's sake," she said.
"You didn't happen to bake a pie, just in case, did
you?"

"Just in case they didn't have enough this year,"
Chrissy answered. No more was said, but Caroline
noticed a smile pass between Chrissy and her
grandmother.

After lunch, everyone brought chairs outside to
the edge of the street to wait for the parade. Soon
other people started gathering, until both sides of
Main Street were lined with a crowd of spectators
three or four people deep in some places. Caroline
hadn't realized that so many people lived in Danbury, but then Chrissy explained that lots of people
from King City and other neighboring towns also
came to watch the big parade. It seemed as if
Chrissy knew at least two-thirds of the spectators
because she kept waving and shouting greetings to
people up and down and across the street.

Suddenly a big roar went up from the crowd,
and Caroline heard the first strains of "Three
Cheers for the Red, White, and Blue." Then she
saw the Danbury High Marching Band strutting
down Main Street, followed by a man whom Caroline guessed was the mayor sitting on top of a
bright red fire engine. Behind him came more town
officials in open-top cars, then some boys dressed

in cowboy gear riding horses, then several home-made floats. Caroline noticed Grandma Madden shake her head with an amused smile as a brightly painted pickup truck rolled by carrying a group of older women in the back. The women wore huge, gaudy Easter bonnets decorated with flowers, fruit, and even plastic birds.

Caroline couldn't help herself as she burst out laughing. She hadn't expected to enjoy the parade so much. Just then she heard a loud shriek in her left ear. She turned to find Chrissy jumping up and down and whistling and waving all at the same time. Then she spotted the reason for her cousin's excitement—behind the floats came the Danbury High cheerleaders, flipping and cartwheeling down Main Street.

It struck Caroline that if Chrissy had stayed in Danbury for her junior year, she would be turning cartwheels in the parade with her friends. *I wonder if Chrissy regrets coming to San Francisco,* she thought fleetingly, before turning her attention to the sweet little kids in pioneer costumes marching proudly down the street.

When the parade was over, the crowd assembled on the school fields to watch the mayor present the prizes for the best floats. Then Caroline watched Chrissy and little Jimmy stumble about in the three-legged race and laughed along with everyone else at Tom's face when a girl beat him in an arm-wrestling contest. Caroline refused to join in any of the events, but she had a good time watching. Her favorite was the hog-calling contest, which she thought was just about the weirdest thing she'd ever seen or heard in her life. *Just wait until the kids back home hear about this!* she thought.

All afternoon Chrissy was bright and bubbly, but as they walked up to the church grounds for the supper and pie auction, she grabbed Caroline's arm and pulled her away from the rest of the family. "I don't think I want to go after all," she whispered. "What if this is the wrong thing to do? I know my pie's not good enough. I know Tammy's will be better. What if Ben won't talk to me? Tell me I'm doing the right thing!"

"I can't tell you, Chrissy," Caroline began hesitantly, "because I don't know how things work here, and I don't know Ben. If he sees you've come because you want to say you're sorry, then that's the most important thing. I can't see that pies really matter."

"But they do," Chrissy exclaimed.

Caroline smiled. "You can't tell me that Ben would choose Tammy over you because she bakes a better pie?"

Chrissy managed to smile. "It does sound dumb when you put it like that," she said. "Sometimes I feel that I don't fit in here anymore."

"You're just nervous," Caroline said. "Look how everybody waved to you today. Everyone is delighted to see you back home. Just go to the picnic and have a good time, and Ben will realize what he's been missing!"

"You make it sound easy," Chrissy said. "I just hope it's as simple as that."

Chapter 8

As the sun sank in the suddenly angry gray sky, Caroline felt her cousin's nervousness increasing. Chrissy clung tightly to Caroline's arm as they slowly approached the recreation hall at the church. Caroline was relieved to find that the picnic was actually taking place inside, because the wind was now whipping up and swirling the dirt parking lot into miniature tornadoes. In front of her, Caroline spotted the ladies from the parade holding the big Easter bonnets tightly to their heads.

"I've got to take my pie to the display table first," Chrissy said when they had finally made their way inside. "Tell me honestly, Cara, do you think it looks okay? I don't want people to laugh."

Caroline looked down at the slightly overdone crust and then at Chrissy's hopeful face. "It looks fine to me, Chrissy," she said. "I'm sure you're worrying for nothing. Ben will be delighted when he finds you've changed your mind."

"I hope so," Chrissy said with a big sigh. "Tell me truly, do I look okay?"

Caroline looked at Chrissy's silky blond hair and blue eyes, set off by the skirt that she had changed into at Grandma Madden's. *Chrissy looks absolutely elegant,* Caroline thought. *Her taste in clothes has definitely blossomed since she's been to California.* Caroline glanced quickly around at the other girls at the picnic and decided that none of them could compete with Chrissy tonight.

"You're the best-dressed person in this room," she said. "Now please quit worrying and do let go of my sleeve—you've almost stretched it down to my knees!"

Chrissy giggled nervously and forced her way through the crowd to the table at the far end of the room. The table already had a good collection of pies on it—some with plain pastry on top, some latticed with fruit showing through, some even covered in meringue. Caroline had to admit to herself that Chrissy's pie did not rank with the best of them—but surely that couldn't really matter, could it? As Chrissy leaned over to put the pie down on the table, Caroline noticed a tall blond girl sidle up beside her.

"Why, Chrissy, I heard you weren't coming today," the girl said.

Caroline took in the bright red dress with the low, lace-trimmed neckline, the carefully arranged curls, and the perfectly made-up face. *Why, that must be Tammy Whatsit*, she thought. *But she doesn't seem like Ben's type at all. In fact, she reminds me of a Barbie doll.*

Chrissy was standing very still, looking at Tammy with a glare so withering that the girl actually blushed.

"How are you, Tammy?" she asked. "Enjoying yourself? How are your rabbits doing? I thought you were going to auction them off tonight, but I don't see them anywhere."

Tammy's face now almost matched her dress, but her smile didn't waver.

"I only came today because my sophisticated cousin from the city really wanted to see what went on at a country picnic," Chrissy babbled on brightly, grabbing Caroline's arm again. "Caroline, this is Tammy—Tammy, my cousin Caroline Kirby, from San Francisco. Her father is a famous music critic and her mother owns an art gallery and they live in the most elegant apartment right on the very top of a big hill. She's been all over the world, but she's never seen anything as quaint as our little church social." She smiled sweetly at Tammy, then squeezed Caroline's arm tighter. "It sure makes an interesting change from Paris or Rome, doesn't it, Cara?"

Caroline shot Chrissy a desperate look. She could tell what Chrissy was doing all right. She wanted to give herself a perfect excuse for being at the social and at the same time score points over Tammy—but Caroline wished her cousin wouldn't use her to score points. She didn't want people to think she was a horrible snob.

"Chrissy, let's go outside again," she begged, hoping that her cousin would take the hint.

"If you want to. We'll go get a drink," Chrissy said loudly, "although I'm afraid it will just be a Coke or fruit punch. They haven't discovered wine coolers out here in the boonies yet!" Then she swept Caroline out of the room as if she were royalty. As they left the table Caroline caught sight of a tall dark figure in a leather jacket, standing a few feet away. Luke was leaning easily against the wall, his dark eyes watching and the hint of a scornful smile on his lips. From the look he gave Caroline, she was sure he had overheard the whole conversation.

"Chrissy," she hissed, "I do wish you'd stop using me for show and tell! I wanted to fit in here, not have everyone think I'm a snobby outsider."

"I'm sorry, Cara," Chrissy said, walking across the lawn to a punch table by the hedge. "But I was only doing that to put Tammy in her place. All's fair in love and war, they say."

"But you know Danbury—whatever you say to Tammy will be all around town in ten minutes. Luke Masterson was standing right there. He overheard."

"So what?" Chrissy asked. "It doesn't matter what he thinks. My family all thinks you're nice."

"Correction—your mother and your grandmother think I am nice," Caroline said, taking a cup of juice from Chrissy. "Your cousin Alice thinks I'm a dangerous creature from another planet, and your brothers think I'm a weird wimp. When Luke tells them what he just heard they'll think I'm a weird, snobby wimp!"

Chrissy looked at Caroline with big, soulful eyes. *Uh-oh,* Caroline thought, *there she goes with her puppy-dog look. I don't have a chance now.*

"We'll have plenty of time to let people get to know the real you," Chrissy said. "If I can just get Ben back first. Please let your image suffer today, if it means I can get back at Tammy."

Caroline shook her head. "I don't know, Chrissy," she said, half smiling. "The things I do for you."

Chrissy looked around nervously. "I don't see Ben at all yet," she said. "In fact, I haven't seen him all day. What if he doesn't even come?"

"Then at least you'll know that he doesn't want Tammy," Caroline answered. "If he doesn't show up tonight, you can call him when we get home and apologize. Tell him you went to the picnic just to see him!"

"I don't know about that," Chrissy said, taking a sip of her punch.

"Chrissy," Caroline said firmly, "if you're not ready to make up and start over with him, then there's no point in any of this dumb pie baking. Now either you want him back or you don't. Which is it?"

Chrissy stepped back, clearly surprised at Caroline's outburst. "I guess I do want him back," she said. "I'll tell him I'm sorry if you like."

Just then, Heidi and Jan, two of Chrissy's cheerleader friends, rushed up to greet the girls. Caroline had met them briefly during her whirlwind introduction tour, but she didn't know what to say to them. She stood by quietly as Chrissy and her friends chatted on about people and things she knew nothing about. So when they decided to go inside to meet up with more friends, Caroline chose to stay outside on her own.

She looked around for her aunt or uncle or Grandma Madden and found herself staring straight at Ben. He seemed to look right through her for a moment, then his face broke into a smile of recognition. "You're Caroline, right? Having a good time?"

"Freezing, actually," Caroline confessed, "but there are so many people I don't know crammed inside that building."

A worried frown creased Ben's forehead. "Is . . . is Chrissy in there?" he asked hesitantly.

"She's in there," Caroline said. "Currently surrounded by the entire cheerleading squad."

"She came, then," he said unnecessarily, as if he just wanted to go on talking.

Caroline nodded.

"Did she . . . did she say anything about me—about what happened the other day?"

Caroline nodded again. "She told me all about it," she said.

The worried frown reappeared on Ben's forehead. He pushed back his hair.

Caroline took a deep breath. "Ben," she began, "Chrissy feels really bad about what she said. She was tired after the long flight, you know. She said some things she didn't mean."

Ben looked at her hopefully. "She doesn't really want to break up?" he asked.

Caroline laughed. "Are you kidding?" she asked. "She's even baked a pie for tonight in the hope of winning you back—and you know what a great effort that is for Chrissy."

A grin spread across his face. "She baked a pie?" he asked. "Which one is it—or will I recognize it right away?" His eyes twinkled as he smiled at Caroline. She smiled back.

"Let's just say you should look for the slightly burned crust," she said. "Oh, and Ben, please don't tell her that I told you she was sorry for what she said the other day. You know what she's like— she'd probably never forgive me."

Ben nodded seriously. "Don't you worry, Caroline," he said. "I'll just wander in there and act all surprised that she's here tonight, and then I might just happen to bid on a pie with a slightly burned crust—right?"

"Right," Caroline agreed, beaming at him.

Ben's big warm smile made Caroline think that Chrissy was a very lucky girl. "Thanks a million, Caroline," Ben said. "Me and Chrissy—well, we've been together for a long time. She means a lot to me. So I took Tammy to a couple of high school dances—well, heck, it was better than staying home and watching TV. Chrissy made such a big thing of it."

"She always overreacts," Caroline said. "You just have to give her time to simmer down. I think you'll find she's nicely simmered by now."

Ben nodded again. "I think I'll go take my chances. Thanks, Caroline." He gave her a big wink as he turned away, and Caroline watched him head toward the church building with large, easy strides.

She looked into her empty cup, then glanced toward the punch table, intending to get more juice, but the ladies minding the table were in the midst of putting everything away. As Caroline ran to catch a leaning tower of paper cups, she realized that the wind had grown even stronger and the air colder. She shivered and decided to go back inside to check on Chrissy.

She moved around the edge of the crowded room until she caught sight of Tammy's red dress. Then she heard Chrissy's voice. "Don't make me laugh, Tammy Laudenschlager!"

Caroline crept closer so she could see the two girls standing next to the pie table. Chrissy's back was to Caroline, but she could see Tammy's bright red face.

"Oh, come on now, Chrissy honey, why don't you admit it?" Tammy was saying. "You only came here tonight to give me some healthy competition."

"There is no competition where you are concerned, Tammy *honey*," Chrissy said icily, emphasizing "honey". "I don't even have to bother to compete."

"You're right there, Chrissy honey," Tammy retorted. "There is no competition between you and me, because it's pretty obvious which of us is better at pie baking. Did you happen to notice my light and fluffy pie right here? Is that pathetic-looking burnt thing yours? Poor Chrissy. Why I remember back in Home Ec when we had to bake those biscuits! Yours fell into the dishwater by mistake, and guess what, they sank!" She burst into high-pitched giggles. "Right to the bottom, like lumps of lead! We all laughed so much! I have the feeling that anything you try to make would sink ... maybe you should just give up trying, Chrissy honey. Quit while you're ahead!"

"You don't know much about me if you think I'm a quitter," Chrissy said, her voice rising dangerously now. "And as for your pie, we'll see if it's as light and fluffy as you think!"

Caroline read her mind a second too late. She reached to grab Chrissy, but Chrissy had already stepped forward and given Tammy a giant push, throwing her backward toward the table. Tammy uttered a loud scream that brought silence to the rest of the room. She fought to keep her balance but fell hard against the table, which promptly collapsed under her. Everyone in the room stood still as statues as they watched Tammy land smack on top of the pies. She sat in the middle of a mixture of fruit fillings, creamy fillings, and light and fluffy meringue, with a look of pure horror on her face. Then suddenly everyone but Tammy burst into peals of laughter, and a few brave people rushed to help her to her feet. But Tammy didn't need any help. She struggled to her feet just as Ben arrived on the scene.

"Ben," Tammy shrieked. "Did you see what she did to me? I'll kill her! I'll make her pay for a new dress! Look at my dress, it's ruined! My hair's ruined! I paid twenty dollars to get my hair set, and now it's got meringue in it!"

"Hey, Tammy, calm down a minute," Ben muttered, looking very embarrassed. "There's no real harm done."

"No harm done? She wrecked my dress! Now I'll have to go home and change! She's even wrecked my pie! I don't know what you could ever see in a creep like Chrissy Madden! I hate her! I hate her! I hope she goes back to California and gets swallowed up by a giant earthquake!"

"Hey, Tammy," Ben said, more firmly this time. "Will you cool it? You're making a big scene here. Why don't you go to the bathroom and clean up. You'll feel better then."

"I won't feel better until I make that creep buy me a new dress," Tammy yelled. "But then I don't suppose she can afford the sort of dresses I like, since her family are just no-good farmers who can never make a dime. It'll serve them right if they're the next to be foreclosed on! I want you to drive me home right now!"

Ben clenched his fists at his side and took a deep breath. "You've a right to be mad at Chrissy," he said, "but you shouldn't go running down her family. My folks are just no-good farmers, too—so are most of the other folks here. Just because your dad owns a feed lot doesn't make you better than the rest of us."

"Are you going to drive me home, or do I have to get my daddy?" Tammy demanded.

"I guess you better go find your daddy," Ben said.

Tammy almost knocked him over as she pushed him out of the way. "You farm boys are all the same," she yelled as she ran for the door. "You and Chrissy deserve each other."

Ben turned to Chrissy, who was still standing like a statue, looking in horror and delight at the damage she had caused.

"Did you hear that, Chrissy?" he asked. "She said we deserve each other. Do you reckon you've led such a sinful life that you deserve me?"

"I reckon I must have," Chrissy said, gazing up at him. She took a step toward him. "I didn't mean to push her, Ben, but she said some terrible things."

A smile flickered across his lips. "And I thought you had a sharp tongue. I think I'll become a monk and stay away from girls altogether."

"Don't do that," Chrissy said softly, "because there's one girl who can't do without you."

Tenderly, Ben took both her hands in his. "I guess we're stuck with each other, Chrissy, whether we like it or not."

Chrissy flung herself into his arms. "I think I like it, Ben," she murmured just before he kissed her.

As they drew apart Ben looked down at the broken table, where several people were trying to salvage some of the pies.

"One good thing," he said, looking at Chrissy and catching Caroline's eye, too. "At least Tammy didn't fall on your pie! Then she'd have a genuine pain in the rear bumper to complain about!"

At that, all three of them burst out laughing.

Chapter 9

Chrissy and Ben disappeared from the picnic, and Chrissy got home very late that night. The next morning Ben called for her before breakfast, and they disappeared again. Caroline was delighted that Chrissy and Ben were back together, but she wished her cousin could spare some time for her as well.

Now I suppose I won't even see her for the rest of the time I'm here, Caroline thought as she gazed out the window at the few scattered white blossoms on the tree outside. *She's probably forgotten that I exist. Maybe I was dumb for helping them get back together—* she broke off that thought in a hurry. *Stop being so selfish, Caroline Kirby,* she scolded herself. *Just be happy for Chrissy, and find something to keep yourself occupied. Maybe you could go to that secret place Mom mentioned.*

She sighed deeply and went downstairs to find her aunt alone in the kitchen.

"So here you are, Caroline honey," Aunt Ingrid greeted her, looking up with a smile from a pile of chopped apples. "All alone for breakfast, I'm afraid. The boys are out with their dad, repairing a fence in the field where we're going to put the calves, and Chrissy and Ben—heaven knows where they are! What a business last night. I don't know where she gets that temper from. Not me, certainly. Thank heavens you're not like her, or there would never be any peace."

Caroline smiled back as she poured herself some coffee.

"So what are you going to have to eat?" her aunt asked, scraping the apples into a big pan and washing her hands at the sink.

"Oh, don't worry about me," Caroline said. "I'll do fine with coffee and toast."

"You'll do no such thing," her aunt said firmly. "Coffee and toast indeed! Your mother would accuse me of starving you."

"But I only have coffee and toast at home, or a piece of fruit," Caroline protested.

"Then at least let me make you some French toast and try some of my preserved peaches with it," her aunt said, breaking an egg into a bowl before Caroline could stop her.

Caroline jumped up. "I can do it, Aunt Ingrid. You don't have to wait on me like this."

Her aunt laughed. "I've been waiting on people for the past twenty years. I'd feel strange if I didn't."

"You should come and stay with us for a while," Caroline said, standing beside her aunt as she dropped dripping pieces of French toast onto a griddle. "Then we could wait on you, and you'd get a proper vacation."

A wistful smile spread over her aunt's face. "Now, wouldn't that be nice," she said. "Maybe someday . . ."

"Why not?" Caroline asked. "We'd love to have you. Mom would be thrilled."

Aunt Ingrid looked down at the griddle. "It's not as simple as that. When you're a farming family you can't just take time off like everyone else. The cows have to be milked, even on Christmas morning, and the animals have to be fed. You'd have to find someone kind enough or stupid enough to take over if you ever wanted to leave."

"You mean you've never had a vacation?" Caroline asked in horror.

"Oh, we've had some lovely vacations," her aunt said. "Usually we go camping to one of the lakes for a couple of days—but a couple of days in a row is all we can manage."

Caroline watched her aunt calmly flip the slices of toast. *Aunt Ingrid doesn't seem to mind being stuck on the farm,* Caroline thought in surprise. *I'd go nuts without a vacation every so often. I guess I take it for granted that I'll be able to go skiing with my friends or down to L.A., and I've even been to Europe. I really have done a lot in only sixteen years, but I always want more. Aunt Ingrid has never had the chance to do anything, and she seems so content.*

Caroline slipped an arm around her aunt's waist—something she never would have done before she met Chrissy. "Maybe one day Chrissy and I can take over your work, and you can go to New York or Paris or somewhere you've really dreamed of."

Just for a moment her aunt's eyes took on a faraway look, then she burst out laughing. "Do you think I could relax in Paris or New York, wondering how you two were keeping house?" She chuckled. "And anyway, what would I do in Paris or New York? I've nothing to wear, and I've no use for crowds. Here—take your toast," she said, holding out the plate. "The peaches are on the shelf. I'd better get back to my apple pies, or the boys will be complaining about no dessert."

Caroline took the huge stack of French toast and scooped some peaches on top. Then she drenched it in syrup and was amazed at how good it tasted.

"So do you have any plans for the day?" her aunt asked. "I reckon we've seen the last of Chrissy for a while. But I'll have the boys take you on a walk when they get back."

"Oh, I'm sure the boys won't want to be bothered with me," Caroline said hastily.

"Nonsense—they'll love to show you around," her aunt replied firmly. "They can take you over to the Mastersons and show you the new little piglets."

"Oh, that's okay. I don't want to keep the boys from their chores," Caroline protested. There was no way she would want to spend the day with her three cousins and Luke Masterson—what a horrible combination!

"Those boys will be only too glad to get out of their chores," Aunt Ingrid said with a smile. "And Sara Masterson suggested last night that I should take you over to meet them all. They have a son your age, you know. He might like to meet you."

Caroline opened her mouth, then closed it again. She could hardly tell her aunt that she was probably the last person on earth Luke Masterson would like to see.

The boys trooped in then and gobbled up the French toast as if they had just survived weeks on a deserted island. Surprisingly, they all agreed when Aunt Ingrid proposed that they take Caroline to the Mastersons' farm.

"Get a jacket," Will instructed her. "It's kind of windy out today."

"Come on, Caroline. It's time for your highlights of Iowa tour," Tom said when she came back downstairs. The other two were waiting outside. The group set off at a brisk pace over the field that separated the two farms. The boys strode through the rutted and muddy track easily in their big farm boots, while Caroline tried to pick her way around the worst puddles to keep her white aerobic shoes mud free. She had thought, when she packed for the country, that she was bringing suitable clothes; she had brought jeans and flat shoes and a poplin jacket, but she realized now that nothing she owned was rugged enough for life on a farm. Her shoes were too dainty, her new jeans showed up the mud splashes, and her jacket did not keep out the wind.

Every now and then the boys turned and waited for her, and they didn't make any obnoxious comments when she jumped around puddles. Despite her cousins' unusual good manners, Caroline was still relieved when they reached the Mastersons' farmyard.

"Shall we take her in to meet Mrs. Masterson or show her the piglets first?" Tom asked, glancing back at Caroline.

"Oh, show her the piglets first, definitely," Will said. "She'll love to see the sweet little piglets."

Caroline couldn't be sure, but she thought she caught Will and Tom grinning at each other, and she decided to be very careful in case they were planning another trick. *I am not going to make a fool of myself today,* she vowed.

The smell of pigs, which had drifted toward them across the open field, now hit them with full force as they came around a series of pigpens. The air was full of gruntings and snortings as fat, pink pigs rooted in trays of disgusting-looking slop. Caroline had not realized how big pigs were when they were full grown. When the boys pointed out the champion boar that had won a blue ribbon at the county fair, she decided it was about the size of a baby hippo she had seen once at the zoo. Caroline was glad she had not opened a barn door on him by mistake.

Suddenly she heard a terrible squealing noise. Her eyes opened wide in horror. "Are they killing a pig?" she asked, her stomach already squirming uncomfortably.

The boys looked at each other and laughed. "That's just the sound they make when they're waiting to be fed," Tom said. "They get kind of impatient."

Caroline decided to keep her mouth firmly shut for the rest of her tour. She just nodded when they pointed out pigs that were six months old and ready to be sold and pregnant sows ready to deliver.

"Luke doesn't seem to be around," Will commented.

"I think he had to go into town. He had a dusting job," Tom said.

Caroline wondered what kind of dusting job Luke could have. It seemed strange that a farm boy should have a job cleaning houses, but she was glad to find him absent.

"And here are the piglets," Jimmy said proudly as they came to another pen with a long wooden shelter taking up half of it. The sides of the shelter were closed in, but the ends were open. In one end, Caroline spotted some straw, but no piglets.

"Looks like they're inside today. It's kind of cold," Will said. "You want to come in and take a look?" he asked Caroline.

"Er, sure," Caroline said hesitantly. "If you're coming, too."

"Climb over the wall, then," Will said, vaulting the wall easily himself. "We don't want to open the gate in case one of them gets out. They're slippery little devils when you try to catch them."

"How big are these piglets?" Caroline asked as she eased herself over the wall.

"These ones—they were only born a couple of weeks ago," Will answered. "About as big as a kitten, I guess." They rounded the side of the shelter, and Caroline caught a glimpse of several little pink bodies lying stretched out in the sun.

"Oh, they are so tiny!" she exclaimed, cautiously following Will to get a closer view. One of the piglets opened his bright black eyes and looked at Caroline in a bleary sort of way. Then he got to his feet and came over to sniff at her shoe. She watched the piglet with a mixture of fascination and nervousness.

"Go on, pick him up," Will suggested. "He won't bite."

Caroline hesitated, then gently picked him up. The piglet gave a squeal of alarm, so she put him down again hastily. The other piglets, awakened by the squeals, scrambled to their feet in alarm, and they all trotted inside the shelter.

"It's okay. They'll get used to you in a while," Will said. "Just go make friends with them. Pigs are friendly little things, aren't they, Tom?"

"Oh, yeah, real friendly," his brother agreed from the other side of the wall.

Caroline stepped from the bright sunlight to the shade of the shelter. The piglets had run to the other end and were huddled together in the straw looking at Caroline with worried eyes, their faces crinkled into little frowns. Several of the piglets climbed to the top of a mound of earth in the corner, as if somehow the dirt might protect them.

"It's okay. There's nothing to be scared of," Caroline crooned. "Here, piggy piggy." She knelt down and stretched out her hand to them. Suddenly the straw at the back of the shelter rustled, and an enormous head rose up in the corner. Caroline stared—that wasn't a mound of earth at all, but an enormous brown pig!

With remarkable agility for one so fat, the mother pig rose to her feet, scattering the babies off her back. She glared at Caroline for a moment, then uttered a fierce roar and charged. Caroline was still squatting down and at a big disadvantage. She flung herself out of the way of the charging pig, falling back into the wet, dirty straw; then, half crawling, half running, she headed out of the shelter and toward the wall. The mother pig was still roaring ferociously, and her jaws snapped just behind Caroline's back. She didn't know whether pigs were just good actors or if this one was really dangerous, but she didn't want to wait around to find out.

I don't care if I look foolish this time, she thought as she sprinted for the wall. *I've just got to get out of here! First the chickens, then Blossom, and now this—three strikes and I'm—*

Before she could finish the thought, the pig butted her in the back and sent her sprawling in the mud. Caroline screamed as the huge animal came at her again. There was no way she could make the wall in time. Then strong hands grabbed her, a voice shouted, and a boot sent the pig backward with a mighty kick. Caroline let herself be dragged over the wall like a sack of potatoes and collapsed, gasping on the other side.

She looked up to thank her rescuer and saw Luke glaring down at her, his eyes flashing angrily.

"What a damn fool thing to do!" he yelled. "You might not know a thing about farms, but you ask someone before you go in the animal pens! You might have gotten yourself killed."

Caroline was already trembling all over, and Luke's reaction made her shake even more. She could see the pig's giant head over the wall and felt sick when she realized how real the danger had been.

"I th-thought there were only p-piglets in there," she stammered. "They said—" She looked up, but her cousins were nowhere in sight.

"Who said?" Luke demanded.

"My cousins. They told me it was okay to go in with the piglets."

Luke looked around frowning. "And didn't it ever occur to you that where there are piglets, there would also be a sow? A sow with a new litter can kill, you know!"

"No, I didn't know," Caroline said, staggering to her feet, angry now. She could feel the mud on her hands and face and the cold wetness seeping through her pant legs. All she wanted to do was have a good cry, but she was not going to give this arrogant boy the satisfaction of seeing her tears. "I don't know a thing about farms, and what's more I don't want to know."

"You made that pretty obvious to everyone last night," Luke said coldly. "I overheard you at the party. You think we're all so quaint and primitive, but at least we can take care of ourselves."

Caroline's head felt as if it were going to explode. "I'd just like to see you in the city," she yelled. "You think you know it all here, but you wouldn't know a darn thing if you ever came to San Francisco. Back home I survive very well, thank you—but then I'm not surrounded by swollen-headed creeps at home."

"Swollen-headed creeps?" Luke yelled back. "Who has been walking around with her nose in the air ever since she got here—looking at the poor, quaint farmers and their poor, quaint little customs?"

"I have not!" Caroline said. "I wanted to be friendly, but everyone here has gone out of their way to make me look like a fool. Well, you might be tough macho guys out here, but I'll tell you one thing you are not—you are not civilized! You have no manners and no feelings, and I think you all stink!"

Luke threw back his head and laughed. "You're the one who stinks right now, lady," he said. "Try smelling yourself after rolling in the pig pen."

Angrily, Caroline turned away. If she stayed a moment longer, she was afraid she might give Luke Masterson a whopping punch in the nose. "You are the most hateful, obnoxious boy I ever met," she said. "Thank heavens I only have two more weeks here, then I'll never have to see you again. Why don't you go and play with your pigs—that's where you belong, isn't it?"

Then she stalked across the yard toward Chrissy's house, fighting the sobs that kept rising to her throat. Her only thought was to get into the house unseen and to throw herself into a hot bath. But she had only gotten halfway across the yard when Luke ran after her and grabbed at her arm.

"Look you'd better come in the house and get cleaned up before you go back," he said. "My mom and your aunt are going to be awful mad if they find out what happened. Your cousins are going to get in big trouble."

Caroline shook herself free. "Good. They deserve it," she said. "And will you let go of me? I just want to go home. I do not enjoy smelling like a pig!"

As they came to the edge of the Mastersons' property, her three cousins were there, lounging against the gate.

"Why, Caroline, what happened to you?" Will asked sweetly.

"You look real messy, Caroline," Jimmy said innocently.

"Did you fall over or something?" Tom asked.

Caroline glared from one to the next. "You know damn well what happened!" she snapped. "And I think your tricks are the most juvenile, path things I have ever seen. Back where I come f kids outgrow your behavior in the fifth gra thought farmers were backward, but I had no you were all as backward as this! And I don't think your mother is going to be too pleased when I walk into her kitchen looking like this!"

"Hey, Cara—it was just a joke!" Tom said. "We're

always playing tricks on Chrissy—she'll tell you that."

"It was a pretty poor joke, then," Luke said sternly. "You know what a sow can do—she could have gotten herself killed or badly ripped up in there."

"We only wanted to give her a scare," Will said, looking away from Luke's angry glance. "We didn't think she'd go and fall over."

"We thought it would be fun to see her come running out with the old sow right behind her!" Jimmy added.

Caroline pushed past the boys, wanting only to be free of all of them, to shut herself away in the bathroom and not come out. Her shoes were caked with mud and dirt, and she didn't bother to avoid the puddles as she strode out down the track. She heard the boys following her but did not look around to see. Jimmy ran past and skipped on ahead, kicking at clods of earth. They were about halfway across the field when he stopped and yelled to them.

"Hey, what's that smoke?" he called.

Caroline had also noticed the black column rising into the clear sky, but the boys obviously ❚❚❚'t.

❚❚❚What's the betting Mom burned the apple pies?" ❚ shouted back, laughing.

❚❚❚That's not coming from the house," Jimmy called back. "Something's wrong. Something's on fire!"

Chapter 10

They all stared for a moment at the ugly black smoke. Caroline felt a pang of fear. She hoped Aunt Ingrid was all right.

"It's coming from behind the barn," Jimmy yelled, streaking ahead of them on his sturdy little legs.

"So it is," Tom said. "We'd better get over there fast. I hope it's not the hay going up."

The boys streaked past Caroline, and she hurried after them, her heart pounding. As she neared the barn, she could hear the crackle of flames.

"It's the henhouse!" Tom shouted.

"No, it isn't—it's Mom's incubator!" Will screamed. "Did you put the latch on the door this morning?"

"I thought I did," Tom called back.

"I bet you didn't. I bet the heater's blown over," Will yelled, sprinting toward the smoking building.

Caroline ran after them around the barn and caught up to the boys, standing together watching the flames licking at one side of the incubator.

"Do you reckon there are any chicks in there worth saving?" Will asked.

"Mom'll be mad if we lose them all after her work," Tom said. "You go get the hose. We don't want the fire to spread in this wind. I'll see if we can get any out."

Caroline thought of all the fluffy yellow chicks, of the special one she had seen hatching out of his shell. *They can't die—they just can't,* she thought. *For Pete's sake, they were just born.* She looked up to see thick black smoke curling out of the open door.

"Can we save the chicks?" Caroline yelled above the crackle of the flame.

Tom shrugged his shoulders. "I'll take a look, but I'm not getting myself fried for a few chicks." He stepped cautiously toward the open door. "Don't you come!" he said severely. "I don't want to have to drag you out as well."

Caroline ignored him and followed. Inside, it was impossible to see through the swirling smoke, and Caroline's eyes began to sting. Through the blur, she noticed that the flames were only licking at one wall and that the table of chicks was almost untouched. She lost sight of Tom in the smoke and pushed forward until she bumped into the table. Then she began to scoop up an armful of chicks, stumbling toward the door with them and dropping them down outside. She was dimly aware of Will and Luke running up with the hose, of shouts and commands, the dog barking, and an arc of water sparkling in the bright sun, before she plunged back into the burning incubator.

This time it was not so easy to locate any chicks. She figured they had probably been as scared by the grabbing arms as they were by the fire and had retreated to the far corner of their trays. Tears were streaming down Caroline's cheeks now, and the smoke hurt her throat. She tried holding her breath, but then she let it out in a violent coughing fit. She grabbed a few chicks, then, feeling the heat beating on the side of her face, she made her way out again. This time she missed the doorway and bumped into a hot wooden wall, standing paralyzed with fear until the wind shifted the smoke and she saw the light outside.

Water sprayed over her as she staggered blindly into the sunlight.

"Here, take these," she yelled at nobody in particular, putting the chicks on the ground and turning to go back in again. A strong hand grabbed her arm.

"You can't go back in there again," Luke's voice commanded her. "The whole thing's about to collapse."

"But we've hardly got any of the chicks out yet!" Caroline shouted back. "I could feel lots of them right at the back. I just couldn't reach them properly."

"It's not worth risking your life for a few chicks," Luke yelled as she shook herself free.

"Just once more, I have to try just once more," Caroline screamed. She ran toward the smoking doorway. This time she screwed her eyes tightly shut, remembering where the chicks were gathered before. She reached desperately across the table, conscious of the creak and groan of collapsing wood around her. Water cascaded in through the doorway and across her face. She snatched at soft little bodies and began to pile them up in her arms, as many as she could hold. Some wriggled free and fell to the floor, but she didn't dare try to find them again.

"Caroline, get out of there," she heard Luke shout from behind. He grabbed her shoulders, turning her back toward the door, and dragged her away. There was a loud groan, and a beam crashed down across the table. Luke jerked her forward, then pulled her out into the cool fresh air as the incubator sank into a pile of smoldering lumber.

Caroline stared in horror, her own tears mixing with the smoke-made tears.

"Can't we do any more?" she asked, looking pleadingly at the boys. "Those poor little chicks. Can't we save some more of them?"

"You crazy idiot, you might have gotten yourself killed!" Luke snapped. "I've never met anyone who likes to live as dangerously as you. And all for a few chicks, too."

"We've put the fire out before it got the barn, that's the main thing. We can always get new chicks," Will said. "Tom's gone to find Ma. That was a lucky escape for us. If that fire had jumped to the barn, we'd have been done for!"

"That was because we did some pretty fancy hose work there, partner," Luke said. "I think we just broke the record for putting out a fire, don't you?"

Caroline looked in disbelief as they slapped each other across the palms, looking really pleased with themselves. She turned toward the chicks she had saved. Some of them were huddled together, trembling in the cold, while others were running around in panic, and still others lying very still.

"Can't we get a box or something to put these in?" she asked. "Jimmy—go get a box, or they'll get trampled on."

Jimmy shrugged. "Ah, they won't be good for nothing anyway. They'll all be dead by morning!"

"Never mind—get a box!" Caroline commanded in a clenched voice. Jimmy shrugged his shoulders again but went to get the box. Meanwhile, Caroline began rounding up stray chicks, seeing them only through the haze of her tears. Jimmy dropped a large cardboard carton beside her, and she started placing the chicks gently inside. Many of the little bodies were already limp and lifeless.

"Don't all die," she pleaded. "You're safe now. We'll put you somewhere warm right away."

"Leave them, Caroline, it's not worth it," Will said, standing over her. "They won't live. They're only chicks, anyway. It's much easier to buy them ready-hatched in town. They only cost a few cents each. It's just Mom's little hobby to do this! We'll get her some more."

Just then Tom and his mother came running up.

Aunt Ingrid stood with her hand shielding her eyes from the bright sun as she surveyed the scene.

"What a mess," she said with a sad sigh.

"See, Ma, we told you that incubator was a waste of time," Tom said.

"It would have been fine if a certain someone hadn't left the door unlatched and let the heater get blown over," Aunt Ingrid replied bitterly. Then she sighed again. "Still, there's no use crying over split milk. You boys saved a much bigger disaster, and I'm proud of you all for that."

Then she saw Caroline, still mud-caked and now dripping with water and streaked with soot, crouched over her carton of chicks.

"Why, Caroline honey, what on earth happened to you?" she asked, kneeling beside her and putting a hand on her shoulder.

"I tried to save some of the chicks," Caroline said softly, trying very hard to keep her voice steady. She was determined not to let her cousins and Luke see her crying like an idiot.

"You went in there to save them?" her aunt asked in amazement. "What a very brave thing to do, but you shouldn't have taken a risk like that."

"That's what the boys told me. They say it's no good, and the chicks are all going to die anyway. I didn't want them to be burned up, but nobody else seems to care." This time she couldn't help her voice from wobbling.

Aunt Ingrid squeezed Caroline's shoulder lightly. "I'm afraid the boys are probably right. Chicks are such fragile little things. It was only my stupid fancy to watch them hatching out. It's much easier to buy pullets ready grown in town."

"You mean all of these will die, too?" Caroline asked, looking down at the few chicks still cheeping in the box.

Her aunt looked at the chicks, then at Caroline's soot-streaked, tear-streaked face. She smiled gently. "Maybe we'll manage to save a few of them if we put them next to the kitchen stove right now. Who knows? Let's take them in the house, and then we can get you cleaned up and give you a hot drink. You look like you're shivering."

Caroline was shivering. All the tension and fear of the morning had finally overwhelmed her, together with the disappointment of knowing that her actions had been for nothing. She got to her feet wearily, brushing her mud-caked hair back from her face. The boys were still busy dampening the last smoldering patches of fire and flinging pieces of timber out of the way. They didn't even look up as she walked past them. She allowed her aunt to lead her toward the house, feed her hot milk, and then run a bath for her as though she were a little girl.

Afterward her aunt came into her bedroom as she was brushing out her hair.

"Feeling better now, honey?" she asked.

"I guess so," Caroline said.

Aunt Ingrid sat down on her bed. "It looks like some of the chicks might make it after all," she said. "There's a few of them eating greedily, and that's always a good sign."

"It is?" Caroline looked up hopefully.

Her aunt smiled. "I do understand how you must feel about the chicks, Caroline," she said.

"Nobody else seemed to think they mattered very much," Caroline said uneasily. "They were only concerned that the barn didn't burn. They didn't even care that all those poor little creatures burned."

Her aunt sighed. "People from cities can't really understand what it's like to be a farmer," she said. "You have to be hard, or you'll never survive. When I was small your grandparents gave me a piglet to raise, then took it away to sell for bacon! I cried myself to sleep for days, but they did it for my own good. Farm kids have to learn that animals are raised for eating. You just can't afford to get sentimental over animals, or you'd never sell a single one."

"I'd be a terrible farmer," Caroline confessed, smiling at her aunt for the first time.

"So would Chrissy," her aunt admitted. "The problems we've had with that girl—begging and pleading with us not to kill the animals she's fallen in love with. There's no way she'd ever be able to marry a livestock farmer, believe me."

"So Ben will have to stick to corn, right?" Caroline asked, sitting down beside her aunt. Somehow it made her feel much better that Chrissy would probably have acted the same way she had.

"Between you and me, Caroline," her aunt said, "I'm hoping that Chrissy will go away to college and find out that there's more to life than Ben."

Caroline grinned. "She's already found that out a couple of times. She's dated a couple of boys in

California—she just hasn't let Ben know about them!"

"And all that fuss she made because he took Tammy to a few high school dances," Aunt Ingrid said, laughing. "What a girl. What am I going to do with her, that's what I wonder. I think I'll do a trade with your mother and keep you instead." Then she laughed some more at Caroline's horrified face.

"I don't think I'd ever learn to fit in here," Caroline confessed. "I would do something else dumb every day. But I suppose I'd give the boys something new to laugh at every day."

"The boys were pretty impressed with the way you went into that henhouse," her aunt remarked.

"Oh sure," Caroline said with a bitter laugh. "They told me I was crazy, and a few chicks didn't matter."

"Boys just like to act tough, especially around strange girls," her aunt said, standing up again. "Don't you believe a thing that they say. Honestly, I could tell they were impressed with what you tried to do." She walked across to the door. "Now I'm going to put lunch on the table, and then I'm going to ask for your help getting my sheets out to dry. I don't trust this extra sunny weather to last for too long even though the weather service says the front won't come through until this evening!" She gave Caroline a bright smile as she went down the stairs.

Chapter 11

Later that afternoon Caroline sat on the porch in the sun, looking out across the landscape. A long hot bath and a hearty lunch, complete with apple pie and cream, had finally soothed away the terrors of the morning, and she was feeling content and sleepy.

The sheets were flapping nicely on the line, making a noise like city pigeons as they billowed out in the wind. Clouds were racing crazily across the sky, sending patches of shadow across the fields. The blossoms above her head smelled sweet, and the flower beds were bursting with spring bulbs. It seemed a miracle to Caroline that her aunt found time to plant flowers in addition to all her other chores, but apparently the flower garden was another of her pet projects, along with the chick incubator. Caroline suspected that keeping busy every minute helped shut out loneliness. She looked out across the lonely landscape to the Meyerses' house, a long empty field away. Apart from that there were no houses in sight. When the kids go back to school after spring vacation, the days must seem very long and lonely to farm wives, she decided.

In front of the house the dirt track stretched out in a straight line to infinity. Caroline stared all the way down the track, thinking about Chrissy and her brothers having to go all that way to school every morning. She tried to picture the same scene when the corn was "as high as an elephant's eye" in the summer. Chrissy had told her that a person walking down the track would be hidden by the corn until he was only a few feet away from the house.

Caroline's imagination drifted, and she tried to picture this landscape as it was when the first settlers came—tall waving grass, unbroken to the skyline in all directions. How lonely that must have seemed. Those pioneer wives must have thought they lived at the edge of the world. Suddenly Caroline stiffened and sat up on her porch swing. She blinked a couple of times and focussed her eyes on a distant moving object. It was definitely a horseman riding down the track toward her. For a moment she wondered whether her imagination had gotten the better of her as she watched the rider, his face hidden under the brim of his cowboy hat, appear from the cornfield.

As the horse came closer she reassured herself

that he was not a ghost or a mirage. She could hear now the sounds of the harness jingling and the dull thud of hooves against packed earth. The horse even snorted once, dancing in place before the rider urged him into a smooth motion again. Caroline watched with interest until she recognized the rider. Then she hurriedly lay back in her swing again, hoping he hadn't noticed her. She didn't want any more confrontations with Luke Masterson that day. *With my luck,* she thought, *I'll be trampled by his horse!*

The horse trotted into the yard, and Luke swung easily from its back, looping the reins around a post with one fluid movement. Then he tipped up the brim of his hat and strode toward the house. Caroline sat without moving as he walked up the front steps. He was almost at the front door when he turned and grinned at her.

"Now that's what I call a much safer occupation for a city girl," he said. "Porch swings do not bite or chase people."

"You should come driving with me and my friends down the hills of San Francisco sometime," Caroline said, looking at him haughtily. "Then you might admit that we don't exactly mind a little danger in the city."

"Is that what you like—fast cars?" Luke asked.

"I'm not afraid of them," Caroline said. "There's not much I'm afraid of in the city."

Luke squatted down in front of Caroline but avoided looking at her, as if he were embarrassed. "I don't reckon there is," he said. "That's why I came over here this afternoon. I figured I owed you an apology."

"For what?" Caroline asked, taken by surprise.

"Because I treated you as if you were a total wimp, and I know now that you're not. None of us would have kept running into that incubator to get those chicks out."

Caroline shrugged. "That's because all of you knew it wasn't worth it. I was the only one dumb enough to waste my time and get my eyebrows singed."

Now Luke eyed her steadily. "Your eyebrows look okay to me," he said. Caroline lowered her gaze, not wanting to meet those intense dark eyes. "In fact . . ." Luke hesitated. "I mean, I think you were pretty darn brave to do what you did. By the way, have you done much sight-seeing since you got here?"

Caroline cautiously shifted her position on the porch swing. "I think I've seen all there is to see around Danbury," she said. "Chrissy has already had me visit all her friends and relatives."

"I could show you some things you haven't seen before," Luke offered. There was a hint of challenge in his voice, and Caroline wondered if the town of Danbury concealed some kind of deep, dark secret. . . . Maybe those innocent-looking houses along Main Street were really illegal casinos. Or perhaps Luke was really a CIA agent. A smile twitched across her lips. Luke noticed it and stood up.

"Of course, I expect Danbury bores you after Paris and Rome."

"I didn't say that," Caroline said hastily.

"You did at the party."

"I did not!" Caroline said firmly. "If you remember, I didn't open my mouth once. Chrissy said all those things. She wanted to use me to put down Tammy. I was just an innocent bystander."

Luke nodded as he digested this fact. "But I still reckon you think we're mighty backward out here," he said. "That's why I thought you might like to come for a little ride with me."

"On your horse?" Caroline asked hesitantly. She didn't want to admit to Luke that she'd never ridden a horse.

Luke shook his head. "In my plane," he said.

Caroline's eyes shot open. "Your plane?"

Luke smiled. "You didn't think us country boys would have anything as fancy as a plane, did you?"

"Your own plane?" Caroline repeated.

"Do any of your friends back in San Francisco have their own plane?" he asked.

"No way. I never met anybody who had his own plane." Caroline could tell by Luke's smug grin that she was playing right into his hands, but she couldn't help being impressed.

His dark eyes held hers. "So—do you want to come for a ride?" he asked. "You'll see a lot from the air you don't see from the ground."

Caroline got to her feet. "That sounds like fun, Luke," she agreed. "If you're sure you've got the time."

Luke shrugged as he turned away from her. "If I stuck around the house, they'd only get me mending fences," he said. "Besides, I like flying. I go up any time I get a chance. I'll take the horse back and pick you up in an hour—okay?"

"Okay," Caroline said. She ran up the stairs to get changed, feeling both scared and excited. She had never been up in a small plane before, and she wasn't at all sure she'd like it. But there was no way she was going to let Luke see that flying in a small plane might scare her. She had to show him that city girls were cool about things like planes . . . *and it will be one up on Chrissy, too,* she thought, smiling to herself as she pulled on a white turtleneck and then slipped her big red sweatshirt on top. She grabbed her wallet from the top of the dresser and stuck it in the back pocket of her jeans. *Chrissy will come home all apologetic for leaving me alone all day, and I'll be able to tell her that I didn't even notice she was gone.*

Chapter 12

Exactly an hour later, Luke showed up again in an old blue pickup. Caroline thought it strange that a boy who had his own plane should have such an old bone shaker of a car. Luke obviously read her thoughts.

"Sorry about my dad's pickup," he said. "Kind of old, isn't it? I bet you drive a Porsche or something."

"I don't even drive yet," Caroline admitted.

"You don't?" he asked in amazement.

"There's not much of a need for it in the city. You can't find parking spaces and garages cost money and there's a good bus system. Most of my friends don't drive yet, either."

"Except the ones that race up and down the hills," Luke quipped.

Caroline nodded. "Mostly the boys do," she said. "Cars seem to be a macho thing with boys."

"So your boyfriend drives the Porsche then?"

"My ex-boyfriend drove a VW," Caroline said carefully, "but it had a Rolls-Royce grille on the front."

Luke laughed. "Hey, I like the sound of that. You broke up with a guy who had a Rolls-Royce grille?"

"He broke up with me," Caroline said quietly, turning away. "I'll go tell my aunt we're leaving."

"Do you have a jacket?" Luke called after her.

"I'm wearing a sweatshirt. It's not that cold, is it?"

"There's a cold front supposed to come through this afternoon. You might need the jacket."

"If you say so," she said, turning back up the stairs, "but I'm plenty warm, really."

"You haven't seen our fronts," he called as she disappeared up the stairs.

"So what are your fronts like?" Caroline asked, reappearing with a light poplin shell.

Luke rolled his eyes up. "Enough to freeze you solid if you're wearing a jacket like that."

Caroline looked up at him defiantly. "California isn't exactly the tropics," she said. "We have cold weather sometimes, too."

"You don't believe me?" Luke asked. "Let me tell you that when a front comes through here, you can be swimming in the creek, and if you're not quick enough, the water freezes solid around you!"

"You must think I'm very stupid," Caroline said. "We do study science in California. I know at what rate water freezes."

"So that was a slight exaggeration," Luke admitted. "Do you always take things so seriously?"

"Not always—only after I've put up with a few days of being teased about everything I say and do," Caroline said.

Luke cleared his throat as if he were embarrassed. "I wasn't teasing about our storms out here," he said. "When a front comes down from Canada, the temperature can drop forty degrees in an hour—and that's the truth!"

"Is that what they expect today?" Caroline asked.

Luke snorted. "What do they know about it? The weather service usually tells you it's going to rain after you've already gotten soaked to the skin."

"Is it going to be okay to fly a plane in bad weather?" Caroline asked. She didn't want Luke to think she was a chicken, but she didn't want to do anything foolhardy, either.

"I aim to get back before any bad weather starts, but the temperature usually drops an hour or so before a storm. It can get pretty chilly up in a plane."

Caroline smiled. "Okay, okay. I get the hint. I'll go put on Chrissy's parka."

"That's better," Luke said, nodding approvingly as she came downstairs in the old jacket. "Come on, then, let's get going if we want to fly around a bit before the weather changes."

Luke zoomed along the dirt tracks while Caroline clung to the side of the truck.

Why am I doing this? she wondered. *The one*

*thing I didn't want was to get mixed up with Luke
... even if he is trying to be nice right now. How
do I know he doesn't have some trick up his sleeve
to make me wind up looking like a fool again! I
wish I felt more comfortable around him. I'd like
to know what he really thinks of me.*

She glanced across at him, taking in his sun-
tanned face, with the handsome, angular jawline
and those intense dark eyes framed by long dark
lashes. *He should be on a commercial for some sort
of outdoorsy cologne,* Caroline thought with a secret smile. *He's good-looking enough. Not my type,
though. He thinks he's superior, the way all these
farm boys seem to. I could never survive in a place
where men thought women belonged back in the
kitchen baking pies!*

"Nice smooth ride, isn't it?" Luke remarked as
they hit a particularly big bump. "This old thing
needed new shocks about twenty-five years ago!"

"Where is the airport you fly out of?" she asked,
wondering if they had to drive the two hours all
the way back to Des Moines.

"Oh, I don't bother with airports," Luke shouted
back over the roar of the truck. "I keep the plane
over on old Schlusser's farm. He's got a landing
strip there that's good enough for me. It's not too
far."

Sure enough, after about ten minutes on a real
paved road, they turned off again and parked beside a hut. Next to the hut Caroline noticed a tube-
shaped piece of canvas flapping from the top of a
tall pole. Luke explained that it was called a wind
sock and showed the direction of the wind. But

Caroline could see no other signs that this desolate clearing was really an airfield.

"Where's the plane?" Caroline asked, wondering for a second if this was another bad joke and half expecting her cousins to appear from the hut laughing at her.

"You can help me get the tarp off," Luke said, walking around the hut to a tarpaulin-covered object. "Here, help me loosen those ropes."

Caroline followed his directions, working as fast as she could so that he couldn't say city girls were clumsy or slow. Luckily her fingers were nimble, and she loosened ropes quickly enough to satisfy him. The tarp slid to the ground, revealing a small blue-and-white plane.

To Caroline it looked very small indeed—not much bigger than a toy plane and hardly big enough to carry two people.

"Climb in," Luke urged her. "You put your foot on the wheel."

"Are you sure it's okay for two of us?" Caroline asked, trying to sound casual.

"You mean we need a chaperone—a boy and girl alone in the sky?" Luke asked with a teasing grin.

"You know what I mean," Caroline said frostily. "I mean is it safe to have two people in it? It looks very small."

Luke laughed as he pushed her up into the passenger seat. "The load of chemicals I usually carry weighs more than you, I'd say."

"Chemicals? What chemicals?" she asked. Luke swung himself in beside her and buckled his safety belt. Caroline watched, then strapped herself in as he had done.

"The chemicals for dusting," he said.

Caroline had a crazy picture in her mind of a large feather duster, suspended from a plane, swooping over rooftops. "Dusting what?" she asked cautiously.

"Crops," Luke answered. "What else did you think?"

"Oh," she said, feeling rather foolish. "Crop dusting. I see now." She didn't want to admit what she'd been thinking, but Luke was still looking at her with a curious expression, and she knew she had to say something. "When my cousins talked about you dusting—I thought you cleaned houses."

Luke's mouth spread into a wide grin.

"Don't even say it!" Caroline threatened.

He glanced at her face and began to laugh. "Sorry," he said, trying to look serious and failing miserably, "but you must admit it's pretty funny. Can you see me flitting around in a frilly apron?"

He burst out laughing, and Caroline found herself joining in. *I'm being too uptight about my image,* she thought. *I'd have laughed at something like this at home. Maybe if I relax and enjoy myself, everyone won't think I'm such a snobby city girl.*

"Ready to see how I do my dusting?" he asked. Without waiting for an answer, he turned the ignition key and the engine roared to life. The whole plane started to shudder and shake, and Caroline grasped the arms of her seat as the plane moved forward.

"Don't you have to file a flight plan or something?" she asked.

"Not out here I don't. There's not enough traffic, and I usually fly too low to bother anyone—except the people whose chimneys I knock off!" Luke joked. "Just kidding," he added hurriedly. He eased the joystick forward, and the plane started to roll out onto the dirt strip.

"So sit back and enjoy it, madam," he said in a hearty voice, "because you are flying the friendly skies."

Caroline managed what she hoped was a relaxed smile. The engine noise rose to a scream, and the plane bounced and lurched as it rushed forward. Then, miraculously, she could see a line of trees and scattered rooftops down below. The plane banked, and Caroline shut her eyes as fields swung past at a dizzying angle. Then they straightened out, dipping and bucking as if they were on a carnival ride.

"Sorry about this—it's the front I told you about," Luke shouted over the roar of the plane. "We're meeting the first of the cold air from Canada."

Caroline took a deep breath, then opened her eyes to see a mass of drifting white clouds up ahead. With the afternoon sun shining on them, they looked like castles in a magic kingdom, and Caroline found herself imagining how neat it would be to dock the plane on a cloud.

"They almost look solid enough to walk on, don't they?" Luke asked. Caroline looked at him in amazement, and he grinned sheepishly. "When I was a little kid I used to picture people living in cloud cities and riding around in cloud ships. Some of those little clouds that scud across the sky, they look exactly like ships, don't they?" Before she could answer, he changed the subject, as if he suddenly realized he was letting his defenses down. "Want to see what my kind of dusting is like?" he asked.

Again before she could answer he put the plane into a dive. As the dark fields rushed up to meet them, Caroline's stomach tossed and turned as if she were on a roller coaster. She clutched at the arms of her seat and cursed herself for agreeing to ride in Luke's plane. What with the pigs, then the fire, and now this, today was by far the worst day of her life.

"This is the part I like best," Luke yelled out. "Is this pretty much like driving down those hills in San Francisco?"

"Pretty much," Caroline lied.

"See, you have to get low enough so you do the job properly and you don't waste the customer's chemicals," Luke went on calmly, as if he were standing at a blackboard in a classroom, not hurtling toward the ground at two hundred miles an hour. Just when Caroline's life was beginning to pass before her eyes, he straightened the plane out, skimming so low over the field that she was sure his wheels would bump against a big clod of earth. They raced toward the row of trees marking the far boundary of a farm—closer and closer, until Caroline didn't want to look.

"Um, Luke, did you notice those trees?" she asked, trying to keep calm.

"What trees?" Luke asked.

"Look! Those trees!" Caroline screamed, waving wildly at the windscreen. She wondered if she should jump out of the plane. She might break a few bones that way, but at least she'd be alive. The trees were close enough now to see individual branches.

"Oh," Luke said, "those trees, you mean." He pulled the plane's nose up so that the trees dropped below their wheels. "You must excuse me, ma'am. We farm boys are a little slow on the uptake," he said with a grin as they rose into the sky again.

"You beast, you did that just to scare me, didn't you?" Caroline demanded.

Luke flashed her a delighted grin. "Yup!" he said. "And it worked, too, didn't it?"

"You never give up with your dumb tricks, do you?" she snapped.

"I just wanted to show you that farm boys can do some of the things your city-boy Porsche drivers can do," he said, "so you don't think we're inferior in everything!"

Caroline opened her mouth to set him straight, but he went on smoothly, "We'll be over the Missouri River in a moment. It's a pretty sight from the air."

Sure enough, as he finished speaking, a great silver ribbon of river came into view, glinting in the sunlight. It twisted like a snake as it flowed between wooded cliffs. Caroline gazed down in awe. The view from up high really was beautiful. She hoped this meant that Luke was going to fly seriously now.

"I thought Iowa was all flat," Caroline commented, "but these look like big cliffs."

"They're more impressive up near Council Bluffs," Luke said, "but I'm not allowed into Omaha air space. In fact, I'd better turn back right now." He banked the plane over to the right, and the river dropped away.

"You want to try flying the plane?" he asked. "Go on, take the stick. It's easy."

Very reluctantly, Caroline took the control stick. She could feel it vibrating in her hands. "Ease it forward and we go down, back and we go up," he said. "Right and left and we go right and left. That's all there is to it."

"That does sound easy," Caroline said in surprise. "What do we pay airline pilots all that money for, then?"

"The one time in a million when they have to land on one engine with half the plane on fire and no undercarriage," Luke said firmly. "Crop dusting is dangerous, too. You get crosswinds that slam you into trees and barns or wind sheers that slam you into the ground. That's why I make good money at it."

"But why do it if it's so dangerous?" Caroline asked.

"Because someone in the family has to make good money," he replied shortly.

"What do you mean—someone in the family? You have a whole lot of pigs—don't they make good money?"

"Well . . ." Luke began in such a way that Caroline knew she'd touched a nerve. "Here, let me take the stick," he said, changing the subject. "Looks like that front is coming up faster than I thought. We'd better head for home."

He swung the plane around. Now that they were facing the opposite direction, Caroline saw that indeed the front had come up quickly. The cloud city had now become cloud mountains, dark and forbidding and directly in their path. She shivered, noticing how cold it had become.

"Glad you brought the parka along?" he asked.

Caroline nodded. "Are those clouds okay?" she asked. "They look awfully dark to me."

"We might get tossed around a bit before we land," he said, "and we might get rained on, but at least they aren't thunderclouds. That's what you avoid out here—thunderclouds and tornadoes."

As he spoke the first of the clouds rolled over them. The sun disappeared, and tiny drops splattered the windshield. Luke switched on his wipers.

"It's colder than I thought," he commented. "And there's ice building up."

"Look," Caroline said, gazing out the window in wonder. "That looks like snow!" "Do you get snow in the middle of April?"

"Sometimes we do," Luke said. "Ah, shoot, it is snowing. I hope it doesn't get any worse."

As Caroline watched, the snow rapidly thickened until they were in the middle of swirling whiteness. The wiper blades worked feverishly, but snow piled up on the windshield. As Luke rolled down his window to try and scrape off the snow, an icy wind blasted into the cockpit.

"Roll down your window and scrape the snow

from your side, too," Luke commanded. "I can't even see where we're going!"

Obediently, Caroline wound her window down. Snow stung her face, and the wind almost snatched her breath away. Her hand was numb in seconds as she reached out to scrape the windshield. The wiper caught her knuckles, and she whipped her hand back inside, sucking at her bruised, numb fingers.

"It's no use," Luke muttered. "I can't see a dog-gone thing."

"What are we going to do?" Caroline asked, peering out into nothingness. Amid the swirling flakes it was not even possible to see where sky ended and ground began.

"Land somewhere, I guess," Luke answered. "We'll never make it back to base. We'll just have to come down in a field."

"Can we do that?" Caroline asked.

"It's either that or keep flying until we outfly the storm or run out of gas, whichever comes first," Luke said grimly.

Caroline glanced across to see if he was joking. She had wondered if he was making a big deal of the snow to give her another scare, but one glance told her he was not. His face was grim and rather pale. His knuckles on the control stick stood out as he clenched it tightly.

"Can't we call for help on the radio or something? They could direct us to the nearest airport couldn't they?"

"Trouble is my radio's out," Luke answered gravely. "I don't normally need it, you see. I meant to have it fixed, but I never got around to it. I think we'll have to chance putting down somewhere. All this snow is making us too heavy."

He eased the nose downward. Down they went, seeing nothing but swirling snowflakes. Then Caroline spotted vague outlines through the snow. Over there she saw a rooftop and nearby the bare bones of a tree.

"I'll see if I can find a road or a track," Luke yelled over the sudden rumbling of the overburdened engine. "Otherwise we'll just have to land in a field."

Caroline sat very still in her seat. As she stared down at the infinite expanse of brilliant white snow, she thought of her parents back in San Francisco and how she wished she were home with them.

"Trouble is you can't see where the fences are," Luke complained, leaning forward in his seat and glaring at the windshield. "Barbed wire can sure make a mess of a plane."

They skimmed over the white surface. Now Caroline could just make out the row of bushes looming ahead of them.

"Luke, look out!" she shouted. Luke wrenched the plane upward. Caroline screamed as twigs scraped the bottom of the plane. The plane teetered, Luke righted it, and then they were bouncing over uneven ground, swinging around in a broad arc until Luke wrestled the plane to a stop. He switched off the engine. Total silence greeted them. Luke and Caroline looked at each other, their eyes conveying messages they didn't want to say. Then Luke grinned.

"Now aren't you glad Iowa is so flat?" he asked. "We'd have been in a real pickle if I'd had to land this in San Francisco!"

Chapter 13

For a while neither of them spoke. The complete silence of the snow alarmed Caroline. She had always enjoyed the snow in the mountains when she went skiing. It was always crisp and sparkling white and looked like a scene straight out of Christmas cards. But this snow was different. It was menacing with its silent swirling—like an alien force that swallowed up all forms of life.

"What do we do now?" Caroline asked in a small voice.

Luke shrugged. "We can't do a thing until this blizzard calms down. We'll have to stay put."

"How long do you think that will be?"

"I don't know," he replied. "Blizzards have been known to go on for days up here."

"You're really enjoying scaring the daylights out

of me, aren't you?" Caroline snapped. "I bet you know we're perfectly safe and the snow will stop in a few moments, but you think it's a lot of fun to make a poor dumb city girl sit here terrified that we're going to freeze to death."

Luke turned toward her and touched her arm, sending an unexpected shock wave all the way up her arm.

"Caroline," he said quietly, "I wouldn't make jokes about a thing like this. People do die in their cars in freak storms out here. We just have to pray that this one stops soon enough for us to find a house or at least a road."

"But the snow can't be very deep yet, can it?" Caroline said, her voice shaking as much with fear as with cold. "It's only been snowing for about an hour."

"Most of it won't be deep," Luke said gently, and she noticed that he still had not let go of her arm. "But it piles into drifts real quick. You can be walking along and suddenly you're up to your neck."

Caroline shivered, and Luke gave her arm a squeeze. "Hey, relax. We'll be okay. Maybe the snow will stop real soon—after all, it is April, isn't it? It's only a freak storm." Caroline nodded, her eyes holding his as if looking for reassurance. "And we can't be too far away from a farmhouse," he went on. "The moment we can see a few feet in front of our noses, we'll head for it."

"So there's no way we can take off again?" she asked.

"I wouldn't chance it today, even if it did stop snowing." He gave a big sigh that suddenly made him sound very vulnerable, like a little boy. "I guess I'd better face it—I'm in for big trouble whatever happens."

"With the farmer for landing on his field?" Caroline asked.

Luke looked away from her. "With old man Schlusser for taking up his plane without permission."

"But I thought you said it was your plane?" Caroline said with a note of accusation in her voice.

"I know I did—and it is mine in a way," he replied hastily. "I mean, I'm the one who flies it, but old man Schlusser is the one who actually owns it." Caroline turned to look at him, and he met her gaze steadily. "Dumb, huh," he said. "It just seemed like the one thing I could go one better than any city boy."

"But why, Luke?" Caroline demanded. "Why would you need to prove that you're better than city boys?"

"Because you made me feel so darn inferior," he said angrily. "Every time I saw you, you had your nose three miles in the air and this expression on your face . . . you know, poor little me, having to suffer with all these primitive people!"

"I did not!" Caroline said firmly.

"Then why did you stand around at the picnic last night with this bored look on your face, not talking to anybody?"

"Did it ever occur to you that I might be shy?" Caroline retorted. "The moment Chrissy and Ben left the picnic, I didn't know anybody. I'm just not the type of person who goes up to strangers and says, 'Hi, there, I'm Caroline, who are you?' Besides, big crowds always scared me."

"No kidding?" Luke asked in surprise. "And you live in a city, too. I've been to Chicago a couple of times. I couldn't stand it. All those people in a hurry—they knock you down if you even stop to look at things . . . and unfriendly? This cabdriver yelled at me because I stepped into the street when my light was green! How do you survive if you hate crowds?"

"Oh, crowded streets don't bother me, because I've grown up with them," Caroline explained. "It's just crowded rooms, full of people like at parties or last night's picnic. I never know what to say, and I always blush and feel like a fool. My mother keeps telling me I'll grow out of my shyness. I guess it must have gotten a little better, or I'd never be talking to you like this."

Luke grinned. "So now we each know a deep dark secret about the other," he said. "Anything more you'd like to confess to me?"

"No way," Caroline said, horrified. "I don't even know why I'm talking to you now, after the way you and my cousins all made fun of me."

"You're talking to me because there is nobody else around and there is nothing else to do and we need something to take our minds off the fact that it's getting colder and colder in here."

Caroline nodded and pulled her parka tighter around her neck. The plane windows had steamed up, and snow was piling onto the windshield.

"It's terribly dark," Caroline said. "What time is it?"

"Only four-thirty," Luke answered.

"That's good. I wouldn't want to be stranded here all night."

"There are plenty of girls who would jump at the chance to be alone with me, stranded in the middle of nowhere," Luke teased.

Caroline had to laugh. "Then go call one of them to come and take my place," she said. "In this temperature, I wouldn't even jump at the chance to be alone with a gorgeous movie star."

"No kidding. I guess this is really torture for you to be stuck here with me, then," he remarked. Caroline didn't know what to say to that, so she kept quiet and waited for Luke to resume the conversation.

"Do you go to movies a lot?" he asked.

"Quite a bit. About once a week, I guess."

"That must be a good thing about living in the city—having all those movies to choose from. Out here one movie comes and stays for about a month. I'd use up all my money if I could see a different movie every night."

"That's what Chrissy did for a while," Caroline said, smiling. "At one point she had seen every single movie showing in the entire city, and that's not easy to do."

"Maybe I'll come back to San Francisco with you instead of Chrissy," Luke said with a big grin. "After all, she won't want to leave Ben again, will she?"

"Thanks a lot!" Caroline said. His eyes unnerved her, and she looked away. "So you like movies, do you?" she asked, changing the subject desperately.

"I'm a movie freak," Luke answered. "See, I've always had this imagination. When we were kids I'd pretend I was Superman all the time. I used to run around with my ma's big old towel pinned on my shoulders like a cape. I even tried flying off the Kirbys' henhouse once and split my chin open. I used to pretend all sorts of dumb things. When I got to school, though, the other kids all teased me, so I started acting like a normal person. But when I go to the movies, I always imagine I'm the hero. Pretty stupid, huh?"

"It's not stupid at all," Caroline said. "Lots of people daydream and imagine themselves doing fantastic things. There wouldn't be any painters or writers if there weren't any daydreamers."

"That's what I'd like to do someday," Luke said. "I'd like to write a screenplay. I have the greatest idea for this hero—he's like a young James Bond, but not as cool. I mean he claims he's not afraid of anything, but you can see that he really is, and he takes chances to prove to himself that he's not afraid . . ."

"He sounds a lot like you, Luke," Caroline remarked.

"Me? I'm not like that at all," he said hastily. "I am the coolest of the cool." He laughed, and she joined in, sensing that he was uneasy talking about himself.

"I think it's terrific you want to be a writer," she said. "I don't even know what I want to be. I spent most of my life studying to be a ballerina, and then I decided I didn't want to after all, so now I'm sort of drifting and looking."

"I bet you were a terrific ballerina," Luke said almost wistfully. "You move so lightly."

Caroline laughed. "You've never seen me dance. And I don't think I looked very graceful scrambling out of the pigpen or running away from that cow."

"When you ran across the field this morning to the incubator fire," he said, "I couldn't help turning around to watch you. You ran so easily, as if gravity didn't mean much to you."

"Really?" Caroline said, half-flattered, half-embarrassed. "Was the fire really only this morning? It seems like that was at least a week ago."

Luke shivered. "We shouldn't have started talking about fires," he said. "I was just picturing a big, roaring fire in the fireplace at home, and it's made me ten times colder."

"I don't think I could be ten times colder right now, or I'd be a block of ice," Caroline remarked. "You know, like in cartoons, when they have to chip the ice away to find out who's in it?"

"I hope they don't have to do that to us," Luke said. He rubbed at the steamed-up window and peered out hopefully. "It's still snowing pretty hard," he said. "Maybe it will be wiser to wait until it gets dark before we leave the plane. We'll see lights from the nearest farm, and they'll be easy to follow."

"Do you think we'll be okay in here until it gets dark?" Caroline asked. "I don't know about frostbite and things, but I can't feel my feet right now."

"Stamp them around," Luke said. "Let's do a dance—sing something."

"I can't think of anything right now."

"It doesn't have to be in the top forty—just sing. How about 'Old MacDonald had a farm . . . e i e i o'?" He started to sing loudly, stamping his feet on the floor of the plane. Caroline joined in, then after a couple of verses she wavered. He looked at her inquiringly.

"It's no use," she complained. "I keep on wanting to sing, 'And on that farm he had a tractor and he came to rescue us through the snow.'"

"Maybe he will," Luke said gently. He slipped an arm around her shoulders. "And in case you think I'm getting fresh," he said seriously, "I'm simply trying to keep you warm."

"Thanks," Caroline said, snuggling against his chest. Normally she would have been embarrassed, but right now all she cared about was keeping warm. "I'm feeling warmer already. In fact, I'm beginning to feel better, aren't you? I'm getting quite sleepy."

Luke pulled his arm away from her so violently that she bumped her head against the cushioned back of her seat. She opened her eyes in angry surprise. "Hey, don't go to sleep," he commanded.

Caroline leaned back and closed her eyes again. "Why not?" she asked. "It would make the time pass quicker and when we wake up, the snow might have stopped."

"But you won't wake up, dummy!" Luke yelled. He grabbed her and shook her by the shoulders. "Caroline, don't fall asleep. The sleepiness is your body giving in to the cold. If you fall asleep, you'll die."

"No, I'll be fine, don't worry," Caroline said. "You see, I'm not cold anymore. I'm warm again."

She leaned against his shoulder. "Tell me a story," she murmured. "Tell me what your young James Bond would do in a situation like this?"

Luke looked down at her head on his shoulder. "My James Bond would have to make a decision right now," he said. "He'd have to do something to get you awake again and then get you to safety." He wound down the window, and snow drifted in. "I'm pretty sure there was a farmhouse one field back," he said. "Remember you saw the roof and then we only just missed those bushes? Well, we'd better not wait until we can see the lights to make a move. I think we should go for it right now. Come on." He jerked Caroline upright. "Come on, Caroline, we're going for a little walk."

"But I don't want to walk right now," Caroline whined. "I'm happy here. You go find the farmhouse and come back when you've found it. I'll just stay here and have a little nap."

"No, you won't," Luke said. He wrenched open the plane door and put an arm firmly around her waist. "You're coming with me," he said.

"Let go of me!" Caroline complained, wriggling to get free. Luke held on tightly and dragged her across the seat.

"I'm not letting go until we get to the farmhouse!" Luke insisted. He pulled her sharply, and she fell out of the plane, collapsing in a heap in the snow.

"Now look what you've done, you idiot!" she yelled, staggering to her feet. "You've soaked me with freezing snow. Now let me get back in that plane before I freeze to death!"

"You are not getting back," Luke yelled back, grabbing at her as she tried to climb up.

Caroline turned and lashed out at him. "Leave me alone!"

Luke flinched. "You are coming with me, Caroline." He reached up and slammed the door shut. "Now you can't open it without the key, and I have that in my pocket."

"You beast!" Caroline screamed, tears spurting from her eyes and burning her cheeks as they fell. "I hate you. If I die, it will be your fault."

"Shut up and start walking," Luke commanded. "We'll head for that dark blur over there. It's either a row of trees or a barn. Either way, there will be a house nearby."

He took her arm and half dragged her through the snow. The pain of the snow seeping through her sneakers had woken her up again, and her anger was now pumping heat through her veins. She stumbled forward, her ankles twisting on unseen furrows beneath the snow. As Luke had said, most of the snow was not too deep—until they reached a deep snowdrift. As they stepped forward, the drift caught them by surprise, and they both ended up with snow up to their knees.

"Oh, great, now every inch of me is soaking," Caroline complained. "I can't remember when I've had such a fun time in years. I think the last occasion was when I got three fillings done at the dentist, and he ran out of novocaine!"

"Come on, it's not far now," Luke urged. "Look, that must be the hedge we scraped."

"Some pilot," Caroline growled. "He can't even miss the hedges!"

The cold wind had picked up speed and was blowing stinging snow in Caroline's face, so that it was impossible to tell which direction they were headed. She could only see a few feet ahead of her and the blurry silhouette of Luke, walking next to her.

"Have you got any idea where we're going?" she demanded, stopping to wipe the snow from her nose and mouth.

"I think we're heading up the track," Luke said. "At least I hope we are."

"Then where's the dark blur you said was a barn or a row of trees?"

"I don't know. I can't see it anymore."

There was a pause. The fight seemed to go out of Caroline. She said in a small voice, "We're not going to make it, are we?"

"Sure we are," Luke said. "Just keep going. We're not in the middle of Alaska. We're in farm country. If we keep going in a straight line, we're bound to hit a road or a farmhouse in the end."

"It's the straight-line part that's hard," Caroline remarked. "We might have been walking around in circles for the past half hour."

"If we see footprints in front of us, we'll know we're walking around in circles," Luke told her. "But I still like to believe that we're walking in a straight line, straight to a farmhouse full of warmth and food and dry clothes."

"It's so silent," Caroline said. "If there really was a farm nearby, wouldn't we hear something? The animals are always so noisy."

"The snow deadens sound," Luke said, "but I do admit that it seems strange not to hear anything."

He reached out and took her hand. This time she didn't fight him. "We'll make it okay," he said. "We are both fine young specimens in the peak of physical condition!" He smiled encouragingly.

Caroline managed a weak smile in return. "Your hand feels as cold as mine," she said. "It's like holding hands with a snowman."

"I didn't tell you before, but I am really the Iowa snow monster," Luke confessed. "This is how I always lure young girls to their doom!"

"Another of your movie scripts?" she asked.

"It just came to me right now, but it might not be a bad idea," he replied. "Peaceful countryside, freak snowstorm, young girl trapped with what she thinks is a good-looking guy—"

"Ha!" Caroline interrupted.

"As I was saying," he went on. "Only this good-looking guy has suffered some strange radiation effects and is about to turn into *The Snow Monster That Swallowed Iowa!*"

Caroline started to laugh, but the act of smiling hurt her face. "Somehow I don't think you've got a title there that will sell," she said.

"Minor details," he agreed, "but you have to admit, it's a powerful horror story, and horror stories always sell well."

"It depends how horrible the snow monster is," Caroline said.

"Oh, very horrible. He eats young girls, piece by piece," he said. "And I'll shoot a whole bunch of close-ups of the snow monster with a human leg sticking out of his mouth!"

"Oh, gross! What a horrible imagination you have!" Caroline exclaimed. "I don't know what I'm doing, alone with a weirdo in the middle of nowhere." She paused, panting. "Luke, I've got to stop," she said. "I just can't walk another step. I can't feel my feet anymore, and I'm so tired . . ."

"Come on, Caroline, just a few more steps," Luke begged. "The house has to be right here."

"Where? I don't see anything. Why don't you admit that we're lost in the middle of nowhere, and you'll survive all right because you're the snow monster, but I'm going to die . . ." Her voice trailed away, and he caught her as she started to sink to the ground.

"You are not going to die!" he shouted. "And you are not going to lie down." He swept her up into his arms, holding her as he would a small child. "I'll just have to carry you, then," he said. "Lucky you don't weigh a lot!"

He started to stagger forward. Caroline nestled her face against his chest. It felt warm and comforting, and she was reminded of the way her father always carried her out of the car when she fell asleep on long journeys. In fact, she found that she wasn't stranded in a snowstorm at all. She was being carried up a long flight of steps, up and up . . .

"But I didn't know we had so many steps to reach our apartment," she exclaimed.

"They added on another floor while you were away," her father's voice said in her ear. "In case it snows. We don't want snow on the carpets."

Suddenly Luke fell forward and yelled in pain. He dropped Caroline in the snow, jerking her back to reality.

"What happened?" she asked in fright as her bottom met the ground with an icy bump.

"Darn stupid ..." Luke was muttering as he hopped around.

"What is it?"

"I only nearly crippled my leg," he complained. "I just caught my shin on something!"

"Let's see," Caroline suggested.

"Not now, we've go to find shelter first," Luke said.

"Do you think you can still walk?"

"I guess so. That darn thing was hard as iron."

"Where was it?" Caroline asked. "We don't want to fall over it again."

Luke turned back. "Right here—look, some idiot's left ..." His voice trailed off in silence.

"Left what?" Caroline asked.

"It's a part of a plough," Luke said excitedly. "We must be getting close to the farm."

He took her hand and began to run awkwardly along the track.

"Hey, not so fast," Caroline begged. "You'll know it if you run into the tractor next!"

"I won't care!" Luke shouted excitedly. "If we run into the tractor, we'll start it up and drive ourselves home. Hey, look over there—doesn't that look like a house?"

Caroline peered through the swirling snow. "You might be right," she answered cautiously.

"I think we made it," Luke yelled. As they ran forward Caroline finally let herself admit that she could see walls ahead of her. They passed a mound of snow with fence posts sticking from it, and then they were standing in a real farmyard, facing a small white house.

"We're safe," Luke breathed. "Warm clothes and hot drinks, here we come!"

As they dragged their feet the last yards toward the front door, Luke suddenly stopped and stood staring.

"What's wrong?" Caroline asked.

"Look at it," he said in a choked voice. "Nobody lives there anymore. It's all boarded up."

Chapter 14

Caroline and Luke stood still as statues, taking in the boarded-up windows, the piece of wood nailed across the front door, the shutter hanging loose on the upstairs window. Caroline swallowed hard to stop herself from crying.

"Why is it like this?" she asked, her voice trembling with disappointment and cold. "What could have happened?"

"That's easy enough. It was foreclosed on," Luke said. "It's happening all the time out here. Families are always losing their farms these days."

"But that's terrible," Caroline said.

"Terrible for us right now," Luke remarked with a dejected sigh. "There's no warm fire in there, and I was sure looking forward to some hot coffee."

"What do we do now?" Caroline asked hope-lessly.

"We find a way in," Luke answered, stepping onto the front porch as he spoke. "Any shelter is better than none. Come on—let's see if we can get any of these boards loose."

"Are you sure this isn't trespassing?" Caroline asked as Luke pulled at the board across the front door.

Luke looked back at her and laughed harshly. "Lady, this is survival. If we don't get inside soon, we'll freeze, and I'd pick survival over trespassing any day."

"You're right," Caroline agreed quietly. She certainly saw the sense in what he was saying. After the struggle through the snow, which had made her sweat, she felt cold and clammy again. Her whole body shivered uncontrollably, and her legs were numb. She stepped forward to help Luke pull, and the board came free with a squeak, sending them both staggering backward.

"See, that wasn't too hard," Luke said, looking pleased with himself, "and I've just thought—my plane is already standing in their field, so we were trespassing anyway. Besides, this place probably belongs to a bank now, so it serves them right to have trespassers." He grabbed the door handle and shook it desperately. The door wobbled but did not yield.

"Are you any good at picking locks?" he asked. "I've seen it done in the movies lots of times with a hairpin."

"Do I look as if I'm wearing hairpins?" Caroline

said. As she shook her long blond hair to show him
that she wasn't wearing any, she realized that it
was weighed down with clumps of frozen snow.

"I hear credit cards work, too," Luke went on
hopefully. "Now I bet a city girl like you carries
her charge cards everywhere."

Caroline shook her head. "You have the funniest
idea of life in the city," she said. "I don't know
anyone my age who has her own charge card.
Where do you get these absurd notions from? The
only difference between us is that we've grown up
in different environments. And right now I'd like
to be back home in my own warm and cozy en-
vironment."

"So you're telling me you have no charge card
on you?" Luke asked impatiently.

"That's right," Caroline snapped. Then an idea
struck her. "Wait a minute," she said excitedly. "I
might have my student card. That's similar to a
credit card."

"Hey, now you're talking," Luke said, patting her
on the back.

Caroline rummaged through her wallet and
brought it out. "At least I'm useful for something,"
she said.

"Fancy student card," he commented, taking it
from her. "Ours are just cardboard. Crummy picture, though. You look much better than that."

"The pictures are always crummy," Caroline
said, noting the compliment. "They tell you to
smile, and then they make you sit there, grinning
at nothing until your mouth freezes."

"And speaking of freezing," Luke said, fumbling

with the card as he tried to insert it in the narrow space between the door and the frame, "come and help me with this. It's so dark I can't see what I'm doing."

Caroline bent down beside him. "Try sliding it up over the lock, and it should spring open," she suggested.

Luke tried it several times. "Well, maybe in the movies," he said with a frustrated sigh, "but not in real life."

"At least I know I'm not alone with a criminal," she said, smiling to make him feel better. His dark eyes were glazed over and his face pale. His body was slumped forward as if he were ready to give up. Caroline realized that, until now, he had been the bright, cheerful one, and she recognized the danger signal he was sending out.

"Let's leave the door for now," she said. "There must be another way in." Slowly she started walking around the outside of the house, looking carefully for loose boards or other weaknesses in the structure. Although Luke followed, she knew that he thought it was hopeless. The last of the daylight was fading rapidly, and the snow was still swirling relentlessly. Caroline pushed it away from her face. Finally at the back of the house she found a small window with a crack across it.

"Luke, come here," she called. "I bet we can get in through this window."

He trudged wearily over to her. "It's too small," he said with a bored sigh.

"For you, maybe. We former ballerinas have

small bones," she said. "Find something we can knock it in with."

The ghost of a smile crossed his face. "I thought you were against trespassing. Now you're going on to breaking and entering."

"I don't care anymore," Caroline said, grinning back at him.

Together they searched the area until Luke lifted an old tractor seat out of the snow. "Stand back," he commanded, and tapped at the glass. It shattered easily. He reached inside and slid up the window. "Do you really think you can get through that?" he asked.

"I can try," Caroline said. The window looked much smaller now it was open. Luke helped her up, and she slipped a leg through. With much squirming and wriggling, Caroline at last dropped triumphantly to the floor. Minutes later she and Luke stood shivering in the dark living room.

"It's almost colder in here than outside," Caroline commented. "I wish we could make a fire."

She looked longingly at the empty pot-bellied stove.

"They didn't leave much behind them," Luke said, looking around the empty room. "Let's hunt around a bit—maybe we'll find something that will burn."

A search of the house turned up two cardboard cartons and a dining chair. "Better than nothing," Luke remarked.

"We can't burn somebody else's chair, can we?" Caroline asked.

"They shouldn't have left it behind if they

wanted to keep it," Luke said with a grin. He picked up the chair and smashed it, throwing the pieces in the stove on top of the cardboard. "Now we just hope it lights," he commented.

"Oh," Caroline said. "We don't have any matches. How can we light a fire?" The possibility of having a fire had seemed so real that she experienced a great rush of disappointment.

Luke reached into his jacket pocket. "I always carry my little first-aid kit when I fly," he said, beaming. "Matches and string and a penknife are three things I always bring with me. You know— 'Always be prepared,' as we used to say in Boy Scouts."

"You were a Boy Scout?" Caroline asked, giggling as Luke pulled out the packet and revealed three beautiful matches. "Somehow I can't see you in that uniform with your knobby knees peeking out of those short shorts."

"I'll have you know I have always had very nice legs!" Luke replied, then became serious again. "I hope this catches first time. We don't have any matches to waste."

Caroline got out her wallet again. "I've got some pieces of paper with addresses on and things. They'd burn," she said, handing them over to him.

"Good girl," he said, taking them from her. "You're sure you haven't given me any dollar bills? It's too dark to see."

"Right now I don't care," she said. "I'd trade money for warmth any day."

"Me too," Luke said. "Right, here goes. Five years of Boy Scout training on the line!" As he struck a match, the shadows retreated to reveal a dusty room with sagging wallpaper.

"Wallpaper!" Caroline yelled. "That will burn, too!" She rushed to peel it off the walls. A small blaze had started, and Luke threw on the wallpaper, a little at a time. They heard a wonderful crackling sound, and flames leaped up inside the stove. The cardboard burned easily, and the chair legs started to glow.

"We did it!" Luke shouted excitedly. "Now we just have to keep this thing going. There must be more stuff around the house we can burn."

With the glow of the fire to help them, they found two loose shelves in the pantry and even pulled the baseboard off a bedroom wall.

"We are going to be in big trouble for this," Caroline said as she helped carry their booty back to the living room. "But you know what—I don't care anymore. It feels so good to be safe and warm—well, almost warm. I'm very tempted to go sit on top of the stove."

"We should take off our wet shoes and socks," Luke said, squatting down beside the fire to do just that.

"I wish we'd found a couple of blankets," Caroline said, "and a can of soup. They would have made everything just perfect."

"It's not so bad right now, is it?" Luke asked.

Caroline glanced over at him quickly. Now that they could relax, she was acutely aware of his presence next to her.

"Your lip's bleeding," she said, noticing the dark stain of blood for the first time.

Luke put his hand up to the cut. "That must have been where you slugged me."

"I slugged you—when?"

"When you wanted to get back into the plane and I wouldn't let you," he replied with a grin.

"I still don't see why you made such a big fuss about that," she said. "We were at least dry in there. We could have waited out the storm, rather than risk our lives trying to get to this place. I was feeling quite cozy."

"Caroline, you were almost asleep," Luke explained patiently. "That is the last stage of hypothermia. You go to sleep and you don't wake up. I had to keep you awake or you would have died."

"Really?"

"Cross my heart."

She looked at him steadily. "So you saved my life," she said. She reached out gently and touched his lip with her finger. "I'm sorry I slugged you in the mouth."

Luke put his hand around Caroline's and brought both hands down between them. "I'm not. It made you angry enough to keep on going," he said. "And you got in through the window, so you saved my life, too."

"So we're equal," Caroline whispered. His eyes, sparkling with firelight, were gazing steadily into hers.

"Very equal, I'd say," Luke said in a husky voice. He reached his fingers under her chin and drew her slowly toward him. Caroline could feel her heart beating rapidly as his lips moved toward hers. Then he brushed her lips with the gentlest of kisses.

He moved back again, giving her a long searching look before enveloping her in his arms and kissing her again, this time with greater urgency.

The kiss seemed to last forever. Fleeting thoughts of apprehension flashed through Caroline's mind, to be overwhelmed by a wonderful, contented feeling as if she were floating on air.

At last they drew apart, gazing into each other's eyes in wonder. Caroline wondered if Luke was as surprised as she at the way things had turned out. Then he gave a little, embarrassed laugh.

"I don't know about you, but I feel warmer now," he said.

"Is that why you kissed me?" Caroline teased. "Just to get warm?"

"That's right," he answered. "I said to myself, Well, there's no electricity in the house, might as well use Caroline!" He shook his head. "No, that's not right. I just can't joke around about things like this. I had no idea this was going to happen, but now that it has, I realize I was crazy about you from the very beginning."

"You were?" Caroline said in surprise. "You didn't show it very well. If I remember the first couple times we met, you yelled at me."

"That's because you made me angry," he said.

"Me—what did I do to you?"

"You didn't do anything to me, except make me feel insecure and inferior," Luke confessed. "I saw you and I thought, 'She's a pretty neat-looking girl. I'd like to get to know her better, but she's everything I'm not—she's elegant and citified, and she'd probably laugh if a farm boy like me asked her out.' "

"I don't believe a word of it, Luke Masterson," Caroline said. "It was probably more like 'I wish that girl would stay out of trouble!' "

"That too," Luke admitted with a grin. "Anyway, it doesn't matter one bit what we thought about each other before, does it?" His voice dropped to a whisper. "We're together now, and that's all that matters."

He slipped his arm protectively around her shoulder, pulling her close to him. It seemed natural to Caroline to nestle her head into his shoulder. She closed her eyes, feeling secure and comfortable for the first time in a long while.

"This is almost cozy, isn't it?" Luke remarked. "In fact, if we somehow found a hoard of food, it would be perfect."

"Don't talk about food," Caroline murmured. "I thought my aunt had fed me so much that I'd never want to think about food again, but I'm definitely feeling hungry. You'd have thought they would have been nice enough to leave a can or two behind them."

"You don't think about leaving things for the next people when you're being turned out of your home," Luke said, instantly serious again.

"No, you're right. That was dumb of me," Caroline apologized. "It must be terrible to be turned out of the place you grew up in."

"The worst thing is that it can happen to any of us, no matter how hard we work," Luke said with a sigh. "We've all had to take out loans on our property to get us through the bad years. My own family . . ." His voice trailed off.

"You can't be in any trouble, surely?" Caroline asked. "All those pigs and that nice house . . ."

"Hog prices are down right now," Luke said. "My mom and dad are worried sick. That's why I took the crop dusting job, because it was the one thing that made really good money." He paused. The fire crackled in the stove. A piece of painted wood caught suddenly and sent up a blaze of sparks. "And I guess," Luke continued slowly, "that was one of the reasons I was mad at you. I thought that city people had it so easy while we were fighting for our lives."

"I suppose we do have it easy," Caroline said, "but that doesn't mean I don't understand."

"You know what?" he asked, turning to her so that his face was very close to hers. "I'm glad we got snowed in, or you would have gone home and we'd never have gotten together. . . ." He kissed her cheek softly. "I think that guy back in San Francisco must have been crazy to walk out on you, but I'm very glad he did."

Isn't life strange, Caroline mused. *I thought the world was over when Alex and I split up. I thought I'd never find anybody who could make me feel special again. How funny that this was the one place I would never have expected to find romance, and yet Luke . . .* She glanced up at him, taking in the strong line of his jaw and the wonderful way his eyes danced in the firelight.

He caught her looking at him, and his gaze became soft and tender. "What are you thinking?" he asked.

"I was thinking that I've never felt this way before," she said, surprised at herself for saying it so easily. "My old boyfriend—he was really nice, and I liked him a lot, but I was always conscious of what I said and did when I was with him. With you I'm comfortable."

His arm tightened on her shoulder. "I hope you're not hinting that you don't have to work hard to impress a simple peasant like me."

She smiled up at him. "Just the opposite. I'm hinting that I feel at home with you, as if I never need worry about anything, ever again."

"I feel that way, too," he said. "We'll just stack up this old stove with all the wood we can find, use my sweater to make a pillow, and go to sleep. Someone will find us in the morning, right?"

"Right," she said, leaning back against him and closing her eyes in contentment.

Chapter 15

"Caroline, wake up!"

Caroline came out of a dreamless sleep to feel someone shaking her. For a moment she wondered why her bed was suddenly so cold and hard and why every part of her body felt stiff and uncomfortable. Then she took in the soft dark eyes looking down at her and remembered exactly where she was. A cold blue light filtered in through the boarded-up windows, and the house reverberated with a loud, pulsating sound.

"What's that noise?" she asked, sitting up slowly.

"A helicopter, right overhead," Luke answered. "I bet it's out looking for us. We should go out and wave so they know where we are."

Caroline hurried to pull on her shoes and socks, then got stiffly to her feet. As she stretched her muscles, she glanced around the room. In the daylight the peeling wallpaper, the dust, and the flaking paint were all too real. It no longer seemed like a cozy hideaway. She looked across at Luke, wondering whether last night had really happened at all. The memory of his arms around her and his soft kisses on her lips brought a rush of warmth to her cheeks. Had he really meant the things he'd said last night, or had they only clung together because they were alone and cold and afraid?

Luke must have been reading her thoughts as he let his gaze wander around the room. "It seems almost like a dream, doesn't it?" he asked. Then he reached out for her hand. "Come on, we don't want the helicopter to go without us." The hand that closed around hers was warm and reassuring, and so was the flicker of a smile he gave her as he led her from the house.

They stepped out into a sparkling world. The first rays of sun were shining onto pure whiteness. Caroline blinked in the strong light, shielding her eyes as she looked up at the helicopter. It was circling above the field where they had landed their plane. She gazed at the deserted expanse of snow-covered fields around her and saw just how lucky they had been. There was no other farmhouse to be seen, no sign even of telegraph wires marking a road. If they had stumbled past this house or walked in the wrong direction, they could both have died. She gripped Luke's hand tightly, feeling that life was a wonderful, miraculous gift. In fact, she felt so full of life and happiness and hope that she wanted to jump up and yell.

"Come on," she shouted, dragging him forward, "race you to the helicopter. Last one there is a rotten egg!" She set off at a great pace down the track, laughing out loud as Luke's feet came pounding up behind her. For a while they ran neck and neck, then his big strides outdistanced her. She watched him running, graceful as a wild animal, toward the hovering helicopter.

"Over here!" he yelled, waving wildly, and the next moment he had plunged forward, up to his thighs in a snowdrift.

Caroline squealed delightedly and ran to pull him out. "I hope you've learned your lesson!" she shouted, dragging him free. "Next time you let me win."

"What do you mean, let you win?" he yelled back. "What sort of women's lib talk is that?"

Caroline was giggling uncontrollably. "It's called equal rights for women to win races," she said.

"And I thought I was doing you a favor! I wanted to save you from the horrors of this freezing snowdrift," he said seriously.

"Oh, baloney!" She laughed and pushed him back toward the drift.

From the helicopter came a disembodied voice. "Hey, you two down there—do you want to be rescued or not?"

"Do we want to be rescued?" Luke asked her, brushing the snow from his jeans.

"Well, I could do with some breakfast," Caroline replied with a grin. "Let's resume our snow fight when we're safely home."

"And I thought you were a delicate, helpless lit-

tle thing," Luke said, laughing as he helped her
onto the ladder the helicopter was dangling in their
direction.

Half an hour later they were touching down in
the field by the Maddens' house. As the propeller
slowed to a stop, people poured from all directions.
"Yeah, it's them, they're safe!" Jimmy was yelling.

Caroline climbed down from the helicopter,
happy to be back safely, yet a little sad that their
adventure was over. She didn't have time to dwell
on her feelings, though, as Chrissy charged through
the crowd to give her a great big bear hug.

"Oh, Cara, I'm so glad to see you! Are you okay?
We were so worried."

Caroline looked at her cousin's pale, anxious
face, then at the other faces in the crowd. *Why,
they all look more upset than Luke and me,* she
thought.

"Come into the house at once, you must be
starving," her aunt said, bundling Caroline and
Luke up with blankets. "You poor things. What an
ordeal."

"Did you crash?" Will asked.

"Did you have to spend the night in the plane?"
Chrissy added.

"Shall we tell them the truth, Caroline?" Luke
asked her with a grin. Caroline felt herself blushing, wondering what he had in mind.

"Yes, come on, Luke, tell us, please," Jimmy
begged, his blue eyes wide with curiosity.

"Well, we decided to take a little trip to Mexico," Luke said seriously.

"You what?" Chrissy and her brothers shrieked. Caroline had to cover her mouth to keep from laughing.

"See, we heard on the radio that this storm was coming, so I suggested to Caroline that we pop down to Acapulco rather than risk landing in a blizzard. We had a terrific time. You should see the tan we got."

"Hey, Mom, no fair, they went to Mexico!" Jimmy shouted.

"They did no such thing, Jimmy," Aunt Ingrid said calmly. "That little plane couldn't fly all the way to Mexico."

"Luke Masterson, you are the biggest liar," Chrissy said, punching him lightly on the shoulder. "I hope you didn't believe one thing this guy told you, Cara."

"Not a thing," Caroline said, grinning up at Luke as they reached the house.

"So what did happen to you?" Will demanded.

"We got caught in the blizzard, and we had to land in a field," Luke answered.

"You had to spend the night in a field? You poor things. It's a wonder you didn't freeze to death in that little plane."

"Oh, we didn't have to spend the night in the plane," Caroline explained to her aunt. "We found a farmhouse."

"Then how come you didn't phone us?" Chrissy demanded. "We were worried silly—we had the highway patrol on the phone all night. . . ."

"There wasn't a phone," Luke cut in. "The house was empty. The farm must have been foreclosed on," he added, taking the cup of steaming coffee that Aunt Ingrid offered him.

"So you two were alone in an empty house all night?" Chrissy asked. Her expression made Caroline glance quickly across at Luke. She ignored the blush that was rising to her cheeks. "It was the only house around," she said, meeting Chrissy's amused blue eyes.

"Wasn't it awfully cold in there?" Uncle Pete asked.

Luke and Caroline looked at each other. "We made a fire in the stove. We had to burn a chair and the wallpaper and even the kitchen shelves," Luke said. "Caroline was the one who started tearing the house to pieces. I was all for freezing quietly."

"Don't listen to him," Caroline said, grinning sheepishly. "You should have seen him smashing the chair and ripping out the baseboard. I hope we don't get in big trouble. . . ."

"Well, you managed to stay safe and warm, and that's the main thing," Aunt Ingrid said, beaming at both of them. "Now, Luke, you'd better go call your folks. And while you're doing that, I'm going to whip up a big batch of pancakes—"

"Oh, great, pancakes!" Jimmy interrupted.

"You have already had breakfast, young man," she said calmly. "For our returning heroes, I mean. I'm so glad you're both back safely. I was worrying all night as to whether I should call your mother, Caroline."

"I'm sorry we made you worry, Aunt Ingrid," Caroline said, looking fondly at her aunt, "but we had no choice. We couldn't see to fly in the storm, and we just had to land where we could."

"As long as you're safely home, that's all that matters," her aunt replied. "Now sit down, Caroline, and you boys go finish your chores. We are going to have a quiet breakfast for once!"

After an enormous breakfast that Caroline would never have imagined finishing back home, Luke made his way across the field to meet his parents at home. Caroline went upstairs and stopped in the bathroom to turn on the bath water. A long hot soak in the tub was just what she needed. But when she got to her room, she found Chrissy waiting for her.

"Some adventure, huh?" Chrissy asked, perching on the edge of Caroline's bed. "I bet you never thought Iowa would be this interesting."

"It was a frightening experience, Chrissy," Caroline answered quietly. "We could have died out there. There were several times when I thought I'd never make it to the farmhouse. Luke was terrific. He actually had to carry me part of the way."

"No kidding?" Chrissy said, looking at Caroline in amazement. "Somehow I can't picture Luke as the 'carrying over the threshold' type."

"I think there's a side of Luke he doesn't like to show to the world," Caroline said carefully. "His tough image is just because he's scared about his folks losing their farm, and he doesn't want to show how scared he is."

"So you and Luke got along pretty well together, then?" Chrissy asked.

"Uh-huh," Caroline said, turning away from Chrissy to open a drawer and take out clean clothes.

"More than pretty well?" Chrissy teased. "So what went on in the deserted farmhouse, Cara? I thought you were my prim and proper cousin from the city!"

"Cut it out, Chrissy," Caroline said, feeling suddenly that her emotions had been stretched enough in the past two days.

"Oh, so I was right." Chrissy smiled triumphantly. "Something did happen. I thought I saw little secret looks between you and Luke. So you two really hit it off, eh?"

"Yes, Chrissy," Caroline said, turning to face her cousin. "If you really want to know, Luke and I did hit it off."

"There's no need to be so defensive," Chrissy said, still grinning. "I mean, it's only logical. You had to find something to do to pass all that time!"

"Chrissy!" Caroline suddenly exploded. "Let me tell you something. Luke is sweet and gentle and funny and creative, and what's more, he saved my life. Literally saved my life, Chrissy. When I couldn't stay awake in the plane because of the cold, he had to drag me out of it. I must have been half-delirious because I fought him all the way. I even slugged him so hard I made his lip bleed, but he still stuck with me until we got to shelter. He is one terrific guy."

The smile on Chrissy's face changed to a wide-eyed look of astonishment. "Gee, Cara. I mean, holy cow! You've really fallen for him in a big way, haven't you?"

"I guess so," Caroline confessed.

"And he's fallen for you, too?"

Caroline nodded.

"How about that?" Chrissy exclaimed, leaping up and beaming delightedly. "I bring my cousin home with me and supply her with the boy of her dreams. Isn't that nice of me?"

"I only met him because you went off and abandoned me," Caroline said, grinning back at Chrissy, "so I suppose I do have something to thank you for in a backward sort of way. Now you and Ben and me and Luke can all go around with silly grins on our faces. Maybe we can go on a double date."

"Sure, I hope so," Chrissy said.

Caroline detected a hesitation in her cousin's voice. "Chrissy," she asked, "is something wrong? Everything's fine now between you and Ben, isn't it? You haven't been fighting about Tammy again while I've been gone?"

"No, we haven't been fighting," Chrissy said, "and I guess you could say everything is fine." She sighed. "It's really hard to describe, Cara, but I just sense that something has changed. Ben has changed, I mean. He's so domineering. He wants to decide what we do all the time and doesn't seem very interested when I try to tell him about San Francisco. He made fun of the art show and the newspaper, when he should have seen that they were pretty important to me."

"Do you think perhaps you just need some time to get used to each other again?"

Chrissy shrugged and turned to look out the window. "I'm still crazy about him," she said.

"Maybe he's only putting down city things because they make him feel insecure and inferior," Caroline suggested. "Luke told me that's how I made him feel before he got to know me. Perhaps you should work on boosting his ego and letting him see how glad you are to be with him again—that way he won't feel threatened."

"I bet you're right," Chrissy said. "He's so darn proud. Perhaps I have been boasting about all the things I did in the city too much. I guess I'll just have to try to be the sweet little country girl he once knew." She turned to smile at Caroline. "You'd better learn to be a sweet little country girl for Luke. How about starting by coming down with me to get the eggs? That's the first thing country girls do every morning, and I'm supposed to be doing it right now."

Caroline started to laugh. "Oh, not chickens," she said. "I'd do a lot for Luke, but I think I'll keep away from hens for a while . . . and cows . . . and pigs!"

Chrissy started to laugh, too, and came over to hug her cousin. "Oh, Cara, I'm so glad you're home safely, and I'm so glad you're happy. We'll have a great time from now on, won't we—you and Luke and me and Ben. We'll have so much fun."

"You bet, Chrissy," Caroline said, giving her a reassuring squeeze. "Only first let me—" she broke off, her mouth open in horror. "Chrissy, my bath! The water must be all over the floor by now!"

Both girls rushed out of the room giggling and knocking over Will as they raced to the bathroom.

Chapter 16

"So do you still think Danbury, Iowa, is flat, boring, and uninteresting?" Chrissy asked Caroline a few days later as they enjoyed a mild spring evening on the front porch. Caroline still couldn't believe how quickly the weather had changed. Here it was Thursday, only four days after the blizzard, and she was sitting outside wearing just a light cardigan over her T-shirt.

"I never said those things," Caroline said, watching Luke's tall, lean figure cross the field toward the Mastersons' farm.

"No, but you thought it," Chrissy said. "I know you pretty well, Caroline Kirby, and I know that you were very bored here the first week. I caught you yawning and staring out the window when we went to visit all those relatives."

"That was because I was an outsider, and I didn't know anybody," Caroline protested.

"And now suddenly you're the local celebrity—the girl who survived the plane crash in the blizzard and got your picture in the paper," Chrissy said.

"It wasn't a plane crash. These newspapers do exaggerate," Caroline said with a smile. "But whatever it was, I'm very glad it happened, because I'd never have gotten to know Luke otherwise."

"Well, you sure looked like you were in seventh heaven today," Chrissy remarked. "And the fuss he made saying good night just now—holy mazoley!"

Caroline hoped the darkness hid her red cheeks. Chrissy was right. All day—in fact, ever since Sunday night—Caroline had felt as if she were walking on air.

"Who would ever have thought that the two most unlikely people in the world would get together?" Chrissy asked. "You and Luke—I'd never have suspected it."

"I don't see why not," Caroline said. "We have so much in common. Somehow we seem to be thinking the same things at exactly the same time."

"What about flying between Danbury and San Francisco?" Chrissy asked seriously. "How are you going to manage that?"

"I'm not thinking about it," Caroline declared. "We have one more week here together, and that's all I'm thinking about right now. These have been the best days of my life, Chrissy. I've been so happy."

"I'm real glad for you, Cara," Chrissy said. "I'm glad everything's going so well for you and Luke. . . ."

She got up quickly, making the porch swing rock forcefully and creak as it did so. "I think I'll go inside. I'm getting chilly. Are you coming?"

"No, I think I'll stay here a while longer," Caroline replied.

"Okay, I'll cut you a piece of Mom's cake for you when you come in," Chrissy said, letting the screen door shut behind her.

Caroline rocked the swing gently and closed her eyes. She breathed deeply, letting the scents and the sounds of the country night envelop her. *I could sit like this forever*, she thought, feeling the warmth of Luke's good-night kisses and his hand running through her hair. *Wouldn't it be wonderful if I could stop time. . . .*

Her thoughts turned to Chrissy and her abrupt departure. *Poor Chrissy*, she thought. *I wish everything was going as well for her and Ben as it is for me and Luke. There's always a tension between them these days. It's clear that they like each other, but something is wrong.*

It had been painfully obvious that afternoon, when the four of them had double-dated. Ben had arrived, excited about the news of a new bowling alley in a town about forty miles away. Caroline thought it was ridiculous that anybody would drive forty miles to go bowling, but the other three were eager to try it out. All had gone fine on the ride there. Chrissy seemed relaxed and sat very close to Ben in the front seat of his big red pickup truck, while Caroline and Luke snuggled in the back. The four of them had laughed and joked and teased each other all the way. In fact, everything had gone well until Chrissy ended up beating Ben at bowling.

"I don't know how I'm going to live this down, being beaten by a girl," he said, laughing. "Just tell everyone we went to a movie tonight, okay?"

"Don't be so sensitive," Chrissy said, still flushed from the thrill of winning. "I just happen to have been bowling several times recently. I've had more practice."

"Yeah—but you're a girl," Ben said, shaking his head in disbelief.

"So?" Chrissy asked defiantly.

"So it would be normal to think that a boy could beat a girl at any sport without practicing," Ben said easily.

"Boy, you have some funny ideas," Chrissy said. "There are plenty of things girls can do as well as boys."

"Yeah, sure—spelling bees and sewing," Ben remarked.

"I meant sports," Chrissy said. "At Caroline's school they have some ace girl tennis players and swimmers and track stars . . ."

"Yeah, well I reckon the boys out there aren't exactly what you'd call musclemen," he said, giving Luke a knowing grin. Luke glanced across at Caroline and gave her hand a little squeeze.

"Let's forget this and go get a soda," Caroline suggested uneasily. "I am so thirsty after all that yelling." Really she was scared that Chrissy's temper would explode any moment, and she would admit to Ben that she had dated some very hunky boys back in California. Ben would hit the roof, she was sure, and Chrissy would lose him forever.

"You two make up right now, or I'm not treating to sodas," Luke commanded. "It's stupid to fight over a little thing like bowling. Shake hands, Ben, and admit that the best man—I mean person—won!"

Ben pushed back his hair and grinned sheepishly. "Aw, why not. I can't stay mad at you, Chrissy. Forgive me?"

"Sure, Ben," she said, taking his hand.

"In fact, I guess I'm lucky to have a girl with a strong arm like that," he said, slipping his arm around her shoulder as the four of them walked toward the snack bar. "It will come in handy when you're a farmer's wife."

"Caroline here has the strongest right arm you're likely to find," Luke said swiftly. "You should have seen my lip where she slugged me!"

"You had to fight him off, eh, Cara?" Ben laughed.

"Not exactly," Caroline said, gazing fondly up at Luke.

When they reached the snack bar, they all ordered their food, then sat down at a booth to eat.

"You're very quiet, Chrissy," Ben commented, taking her hand.

"I was just thinking that in ten days' time, we'll be back in California," she said.

"Don't mention that, please," Ben said, holding her tightly. "I don't know that I can bear to let you go again. I just have to keep on telling myself that it's almost over now. Only May and June, and then you'll be home for good. Then we'll be back together all the time."

"Er, sure, Ben," Chrissy said.

"And only one more year of school, then we're free!" he went on. "How about that, Chrissy? One more year, then we can think about getting married."

"Hey, hold on a minute," Chrissy said. "I'm not ready to think about stuff like that yet. I've got lots of things to do before I settle down. I've got to travel some more and go to college . . ."

"College? What do you want to go to college for, girl?" Ben asked in surprise.

"To finish my education," Chrissy replied calmly.

"Then you can go to the community college over in Huntsville. They have bookkeeping and stuff that could be useful, though I don't know why you'd want to bother."

"I mean a real college, maybe even a big university," Chrissy said. "I'm not sure what I want to study yet, but it won't be bookkeeping. I'm thinking about becoming a veterinarian or maybe a journalist."

"You mean a career?" he demanded. "A farmer's wife's not good enough for you?"

"No, Ben," Chrissy said emphatically. "It's not good enough for me. I want to be a person—maybe a married person, but a person in my own right."

They had dropped the subject after that, but Caroline could see that Ben was hurt and that Chrissy, in a way, was hurt, too.

Caroline shivered, feeling a cool breeze invade the tranquillity of the porch. She got up and slipped quietly inside to find Chrissy sitting alone in the kitchen, a large slice of apple cake uneaten in front of her.

"Your cake is here," Chrissy said. "There's cream in the fridge if you want."

Caroline took the cake and sat down opposite her cousin. Chrissy looked up and sighed unhappily. "Cara, what am I going to do?"

"About Ben?"

Chrissy nodded. "Remember when I told you that he'd changed? I was wrong. He's the same way he always was. I'm the one who's changed." She sank her chin into her hand and looked down at the checkered tablecloth. "Before I went away everything he said seemed to make sense. I thought the best thing in the world would be to marry him and move across to his farm."

"But now you're not sure of that anymore," Caroline said softly.

"I'm not sure of anything anymore," Chrissy said with another big sigh. "I don't even know what I want from life, but I do know that I want something more than my mother has. She's happy enough, I know, but I wouldn't be. I'm just not good at playing second fiddle." She looked up suddenly and smiled. "You know me—can you imagine me waiting hand and foot on any man?"

"Frankly, no," Caroline said, grinning.

"And that's what Ben expects from a wife. You saw today. He wants to be head honcho all the time."

"He may grow out of it," Caroline said. "Maybe he'll go to college and learn that there's more to life than the Danbury football team."

"But what do I do now?" Chrissy asked.

"Do you want to break off with him?"

"I think I still love him, that's the trouble," Chrissy said. "We've been together for three years. That's a lot to throw away all at once."

"Then maybe you should wait and see," Caroline suggested. "You may both have to make some compromises that you don't like if you want to stay together—or maybe sticking with Ben won't be worth the sacrifices. I think by the time you have to make a decision, you'll already know the answer."

Chrissy got up and walked nervously around the table. "All this romance and love business—it's so hard, isn't it?" she asked. "I mean, trying to find the perfect boy. How do you ever know when you've found him? What if you break up and he was the right one, and you end up becoming an old maid with only your cats for company?"

Caroline turned around and laughed. "Oh, Chrissy, you are funny. As if you could ever become an old maid. You'll always have guys lining up to go out with you. And you're only just sixteen—you have years and years ahead before you have to start worrying about the future. Just enjoy today— that's what I'm trying to do." Suddenly she turned serious. "I think Luke is the most wonderful boy I could ever meet, but I'm not going to let myself get depressed because we've only got a few more days together." Caroline said the words with a confidence she didn't feel inside. In only ten days she would have to decide her own future—would it include Luke Masterson?

Chrissy obviously wasn't fooled by Caroline's bravado. "I know you better than to believe that baloney, Cara," she said, sitting beside her cousin. "And I understand if you don't want to talk about it, but just remember that besides being a good talker, I can be a good listener sometimes, too."

"Thanks, Chrissy," Caroline said. "Isn't it strange? I came here to help you solve your boy problems, but instead I got one of my own."

"Well, at least we accomplished one of our original goals here," Chrissy remarked.

"What's that?"

Chrissy grinned mischievously. "I got back at Tammy Laudenschlager. It was a spectacular fall, wasn't it?"

"Very."

The smile spread over Chrissy's face, lighting up her eyes. "It was worth coming here for that alone," she said. "Come on, Cara, let's get some cream for that cake."

The days rushed by quickly after that, as if they were caught in a machine where time could be speeded up. Caroline tried, but she couldn't shut out thoughts about what would happen in a few short days. School started at Danbury High that Monday, and Chrissy took Caroline back to her old school. During the lunch break, the kids gathered around Chrissy and Caroline, asking all kinds of questions about life in California. Although Caroline had already heard lots of funny questions from Chrissy's relatives, she wasn't prepared for some of the absurd notions that the Danbury kids had. They seemed to assume that Caroline spent her days soaking in a hot tub, taking drugs, or drinking wine, when she wasn't meeting movie stars, being mugged, or getting involved in a demonstration on a city street. She recalled the funny ideas that she and her friends had had about farm life and decided that there should be an exchange program between city kids and farm kids, like there was between different countries.

With Luke back in school full-time, Caroline was already experiencing the first pangs of separation. For a few wonderful days they had shared every moment together. Now she had to wait for school bells to give them fleeting moments together, and each new parting reminded her that soon she would be a thousand miles away.

On the day before she was due to leave, Luke met her at the Madden farm right after school.

"Do you want to go anywhere special?" he asked, his forehead wrinkling into a frown. "I'd like to take you somewhere really nice on your last day here. Unfortunately the French restaurant in town is closed at the moment, and so are the night club and theater. . . ." He managed a big smile.

Caroline slipped her hand into his. "Let's just go for a walk," she said, "so we can be completely alone. My aunt's house is frantic with Chrissy packing and all the relatives stopping by."

"Okay. I know a good place I'd like to show you," Luke said. "It's a fair way off, though."

"I don't mind walking. In the city we nearly always walk everywhere."

"That's great, then," Luke said, beaming at her. "It's a nice afternoon for walking."

It was, Caroline thought, a perfect afternoon for walking. For once the wind had dropped, the sun was shining, and it was as warm as early summer. New growth seemed to have sprouted everywhere along the narrow path between the fields. Bright early flowers displayed their glorious colors, bees buzzed sleepily, and birds sung like crazy from every tree. A rabbit sat up to watch them, then hopped away. *And I had thought this place was bleak and desolate,* Caroline marveled. During the three weeks she'd been there, the Iowa countryside had transformed itself into a springtime wonderland full of life.

They walked down the track, talking about little things—what had happened in math class and the upcoming baseball game. Finally they came to a line of trees, willows dressed in bright new green, that bordered a little creek. The creek was running full to the brim after last week's snow. It gurgled and murmured as it skipped brightly along. Luke ducked under a willow branch and led Caroline along a narrow footpath beside the stream. They walked in single file, not talking at all, cut off from the world by the row of willows until they came to a small circle of grass, surrounded by big willow trees, sloping down to the water's edge.

"This is the place I wanted to show you," Luke said, sinking onto a big log. "I used to come here a lot when I was a little kid and wanted to be alone."

He took Caroline's hand and pulled her down onto the log, close beside him. Caroline sat there, soaking in the warmth of the sun, the hum of insects, the soft whisper of the water. The willows formed a dense screen behind them, while tall rushes hid the other side of the bank. The place seemed strangely familiar to Caroline. "I can't help feeling that I've seen this place before," she said. "But I couldn't have, could I?"

"Unless I conjured you up in one of my daydreams," Luke said, smiling as he stroked her cheek playfully.

"I think I know now," she said excitedly. "I think this must be my mother's secret place that she told me about. She used to come here a lot when she was growing up in Danbury."

"See, I knew we were meant for each other," Luke said, gazing into her eyes. "Our families are already linked by the same secret place." Then his smile clouded over, and he gave her hand a little squeeze. "Oh, Cara, what are we going to do about us?"

"What can we do?" she asked hopelessly.

"I just can't let you go," Luke said. "You are the most special girl I've ever met."

"And you are the most special boy."

"Then we'll have to find a way to be together somehow."

"But where, Luke? Where would it ever work?"

His face lit up with inspiration. "I know—you

could do what Chrissy did next year. You could come and live here."

"I couldn't do that," Caroline said with a sigh. "I do want to be with you, but I couldn't give up my senior year at home. There are so many courses they offer at my school and don't offer here, and it's important to me to get into a good college."

"Then I'll have to get a job in San Francisco in the summer. What do you think a farm boy like me could do in the city?"

"Luke," she whispered, taking his hand in both of hers, "you'd hate it in the city. All those people in a hurry and the noise, you'd feel trapped there."

"I know," he said, "but I'd do it for you."

Caroline slid her arms around his neck. "I don't want you to do it for me."

"Well, what are we going to do, then? You sound as if you don't want to see me again," he said, his voice rising.

"You know that I do," Caroline said. "I just can't see right now how we can be together. We don't belong anywhere, you and I."

He held her close to him. "We'll make somewhere," he said. "Write to me, won't you, and maybe you can come out again in the summer, or I'll come to you. I'll survive okay in the city for a week or two."

"We can do all that," Caroline said, "but I get the scary feeling that it will never be the same again. This was like a magic time, wasn't it? Just you and me in our own world. I don't know if we could ever create that world again. Next time we meet things will be different. . . ."

"I love you, Caroline," Luke whispered, "and it's going to take more than a little problem like a thousand miles and two opposite ways of life to put me off!"

"Oh, Luke," she said, feeling the tears welling up in her eyes, "I love you, too."

His mouth came to meet hers. She closed her eyes and responded to his kisses, holding him tightly and shutting all thoughts from her mind until she was again floating in the warmth and happiness of being with him. When the kiss finally ended, she noticed a small tear trickling down his cheek. She reached up to wipe it away. Luke grinned with embarrassment. "Don't let old Ben know. He'd never quit teasing me," he said.

"Old Ben is about to lose his girlfriend because he tries to be too macho," Caroline said.

"No kidding. They're not going to break up, are they?"

"Not now, but I don't think they'll be together much longer. Chrissy has seen that there's more to life than being a farmer's wife."

"I don't think it would be such a bad life," Luke said, gazing at her wistfully. "If the farmer was also a writer and they found a little farm just a couple of miles from San Francisco . . ."

"And they kept no pigs, cows, or chickens!" Caroline finished for him, starting to laugh.

"Agreed," Luke said. "No pigs, cows, or chickens. I never did like those things, anyway—too much hard work! How about we grow Christmas trees? You just plant them, and five years later you sell them."

"That sounds more like my kind of farming," Caroline replied. "As long as the farmer didn't mind his wife going off into the city every day to pursue her career. . . ."

"You see—maybe thing can work out okay," Luke said, his face glowing like a little boy's after his first home run. "Can I write to you, anyway, Cara? I want to share my ideas with you—all the things I can't tell people around here."

"I'd like that," Caroline said.

He stood up slowly. "I hate to say this, but maybe we should be getting back. They've planned that big farewell dinner for you tonight. I suppose you ought to be there!"

"Are you coming?" she asked.

"I don't think I will," he said slowly. "I'd rather say good-bye to you now, while we're alone." He took her into his arms again. "Good-bye Caroline," he whispered.

"Good-bye Luke."

Moments later they walked from the secret place out into the setting sun and back to the real world.

Chapter 17

The plane dipped a wing as it swung toward the west after take-off. Chrissy was still pressed against the window, waving madly.

"Bye, everyone, bye!" she was yelling.

Caroline tapped her arm. "Chrissy, they can't see you anymore."

"I know," Chrissy said with a smile, "but it makes me feel better, and I bet I'm transferring my thought waves down to them."

"The way you're yelling, you don't need to bother with thought waves," Caroline said dryly. "Half the state of Iowa can hear you."

Chrissy glanced at the amused faces of the people in the seats around her. "Sorry," she said to Caroline. "I always get carried away at hellos and good-byes. I can't be quiet and well behaved like you. . . ." She eyed Caroline steadily. "You know, I don't think my mother was entirely joking when she suggested that we swap, me and you. You might not think that was such a bad idea now. . . ."

Caroline smiled wistfully. "I couldn't live out here, Chrissy. I'm just not a country person. All this space overwhelms me, and I'll never get used to the chickens or the pigs . . ."

"But what about Luke? Wouldn't he be worth sticking around for?"

Caroline gave a long sigh. "I wish I could shrink Luke down and put him in a little box and carry him around with me," she said. "That would be perfect."

"I hope you could unshrink him again whenever you needed to," Chrissy remarked. "I bet he wouldn't be nearly as fun if he were only two inches tall."

Caroline giggled. "Of course I'd be able to unshrink him. Every day when I got home from school, I'd just—" She broke off, turning away to stare out of the window. "It's so far away, Chrissy," she said in a voice dangerously close to tears.

"I know," Chrissy agreed.

"It's so dumb, really," Caroline went on. "It's one of those things that never should have happened, because nothing could ever become of it. I should have known that from the beginning, back in that empty house, and told him. . . ."

"Do you really wish you'd never got started with him?" Chrissy asked. "Weren't the last two weeks worth it?"

Caroline nodded. 'Yes, they were. I wouldn't

have traded a single moment. If I never see him again in my whole life, I'll always remember . . ." She turned to the window again. She didn't want Chrissy to see the tears she couldn't hold back.

"Look," she said. "There's the Missouri River. I flew over it with Luke, only much closer to the ground." Way down below them Caroline could see a small plane flying, making a tiny black cross of shadow on the flat fields. Caroline stared at it as if hypnotized. The small plane seemed to be going so slowly, hovering like an insect as they passed over it. She couldn't even see if it was blue and white, but she waved anyway.

"You just told me nobody could see me when I waved," Chrissy said.

"I know," Caroline said, "but it makes me feel better somehow."

"We're past the river now," Chrissy exclaimed, leaning across Caroline. "That means we're out of Iowa and heading back for the Golden Gate! Think of it, Cara—pizza whenever we want and a whole ton of new movies to see. And all the kids at school will be waiting to hear all about our trip. I hope your parents are in the mood for Chinese food when we get home—ooh, and a hot-fudge sundae for dessert! California, here we come!!"

She threw her arm around Caroline's shoulder, and Caroline looked away from the window, not knowing whether to laugh or cry.

Here's a sneak preview of *Flip Side,* book number six in the continuing SUGAR & SPICE series from Ivy Books.

"So when do I get to meet Jeff?" Chrissy asked Caroline.

Caroline made a face. "I don't know if I'll let you meet him ever," she said.

"Meaning what?"

"Meaning that I know you, Chrissy Madden. You'll start flirting with him instantly and before I know it, you'll have lured him away."

Chrissy grinned broadly. "So you are getting interested in him after all?" she asked. "All that pretending he meant nothing to you was just a bluff?"

"I don't know whether I feel anything for him or not, Chrissy," Caroline answered. "We've only been out together twice and in the store we're too busy to talk most of the time."

"Well, if you don't let me meet him soon, I'll start creeping down to the store and spying on you, Chrissy warned.

"You'd better not," Caroline said. "Knowing you, you'd probably knock over a drum set worth a few thousand."

"I would not, Caroline. You make me sound as bad as Roger."

"He can't be too bad," Caroline remarked, "or you'd never have gone out for pizza with him. Or was the pizza only out of pity?"

"No, of course it wasn't," Chrissy protested. She'd had a lot of fun with Roger that night. Talking to him had reminded her of a regular dinner table conversation back home.

ABOUT THE AUTHOR

Janet Quin-Harkin is the author of more than thirty books for young adults, including the best-selling *Ten-Boy Summer* and *On Our Own*, its sequel series. Ms. Quin-Harkin lives just outside of San Francisco with her husband, three teenage daughters, and one son.